Plan B Drama & Baby Mama's 2

S.L. Partee

Plan B Drama & Baby Mama's 2

Mailing List

To stay up to date on new releases, plus get information on contests, sneak peeks, and more,

Go To The Website Below...

www.colehartsignature.com

To Nyiesha Williams, a true angel on earth.

Contact the Author
Facebook: Author Stephanie L. Partee
IG and all other platforms: Author_SLPartee

Chapter 1
Lishan Grey

My shoulder had to be on fire from the blaze in my chest. Groaning from the agonizing pain, I rolled my head alongside the cold kitchen tile. My fingertips brushed against the knot resting on the back of my head while I did my best to mobilize myself. There was a phone chiming, but it was hard to move. For a moment, it stopped, but then it started again. My phone was still in the pocket of my jacket, but that wasn't what was going off. The sight of all the blood when I opened my eyes sent them rolling back with sudden chills sweeping over me. Before curling up and allowing darkness to swallow me, I hugged myself tighter.

"Shit!" Wood's deep, panicked voice jolted me awake.

I wasn't sure how much time had passed, but I was weak and confused. It was hard to tell if he was there or if he was a figment of my imagination. His strong arms pulled me closer, and the pressure against my shoulder sent me screaming in pain as both eyes popped open. *This was damn sure real.* Hovering over me with traces of worry flitting through his enamoring orbs, in that moment, one thing became clear: he cared. Cradling me close to his chest, he rocked me before swaddling me into his large arms and rushing me out of the house.

"I got you, shorty. Just hold on for me, aight?" he pleaded.

My eyes fluttered inconsistently throughout the ride. It was bumpy due to Wood yanking the wheel through traffic like a NASCAR driver.

"What the fuck happened?" Wylde's panicked tone was all I made out as his profile in the passenger's seat came into view. "How the fuck he get to both of the fucking guards!"

"Shayne," I muttered.

When I was dropped onto the gurney and rushed through the sliding doors of the hospital emergency room, my eyes fell on the white lights above me. Doctors and nurses surrounded me, calling out jargon I didn't recognize while wheeling me along.

"What's the patient's name?" I heard a nurse ask.

When I managed to glance above my head, I found Wood there, eyes flooded with concern as he followed us closely through the halls.

"Lishan Grey," he told them.

"Lishan, hey, you're at the hospital. We are taking you up to emergency surgery. Is there anything else you can tell us?" the nurse queried, leaning toward me with warm hazel eyes.

"I'm pregnant," I mumbled, removing the oxygen mask from my face. "I think. I took a home test." I caught one last glimpse of Wood's face, which was now covered in shock.

"Okay, we are going to check your blood work for you as well, but we have to get you to surgery. Sir, you are going to have to wait in the waiting room. Has her family been notified?"

"No." I reached for the nurse's wrist, and she paused with a skeptical stare.

"Honey, it's protocol—"

"My grandfather, he's very sick, and... my siblings, I don't want to worry them. They're just kids."

"I have to do my job. It's going to be fine," she assured, but she had no idea the can of worms she was opening.

Growing dizzy and nauseous, I took in the room spinning before my head slipped to one side and my eyes closed.

A couple of hours later...

The sterile hospital smell was overwhelming when I finally came around. Low lighting in the room had me squinting. Grogginess filled my head. I was high off the good shit as my eyes adjusted. Propped up against a few pillows, my gaze managed to fall to the bracelet on my wrist. What caught me off guard was Misael in a wheelchair beside my bed, his oxygen tank right beside him as he dozed. Licking my lips, I attempted to speak and realized how dry my throat was. Wincing from the ache in my shoulder, the rest of my body followed suit in pain.

"Hey, old man," I croaked, causing his head to lift as a lazy smile fell on his lips.

He was only seventy-one years old, but he seemed so much older due to his illness.

"I told them not to call you."

"And I'm sure nobody in here wanted to lose they job listening to you." His words were slow because they winded him, and it reminded me that he was the one on borrowed time.

"Where are the kids?" I asked, brows furrowing as he reached for the water pitcher and plastic cup.

"In the hallway."

"They shouldn't be here. You shouldn't be here," I said just as my door swung open.

"Lishan!" The three beats to my heart saw that I was awake and fell over each other, trying to get to me.

"Now y'all be careful. She's fragile right now," Misael warned.

Taking heed to his advice, they each paused and decided to take turns giving me light hugs and displays of affection while surrounding me on the opposite side of my bed. Following right behind them, with a presence as large as a fifty-foot building, Wood lingered as the door shut behind him.

"I'm not fragile," I argued as Lumi rested her head against my chest.

"I'm so glad you and the baby are okay," she gushed, sending my heart racing.

I was still a little discombobulated from everything, and the drugs weren't helping as I recalled all that happened leading up to me being in this bed.

"Yeah, the doctor confirmed for us." Misael shook his head. "I don't know what to say, Lishan."

"Me either. That's why I didn't say anything, Pop. I was going to the doctor, and then... I don't know." The weight of Wood's stare was staggering, taking air from me the longer he scrutinized me.

He had never seen me like that before. I was a natural nurturer, regardless of how I played it. Taking care of them had been my job for the last seven years, and I took it very seriously.

"I can't wait to be an auntie," my little sister jovially carried on.

Ledger smacked his lips and gave an eye roll. "Yeah, right. You think she's keeping a baby? She can barely take care of us by herself."

"Where else would the baby go?" My nine-year-old sister seemed confused by the statement as her big doe eyes searched mine.

"Ledger," I warned, but there was something in his demeanor that told me he was on some other type of time.

"What? Am I supposed to sit here and keep pretending still?"

"Listen here, little boy—" Misael started coughing, and I threw my head back onto the pillows as my blood pressure started to rise on the machine beside the bed.

"I ain't no little boy! I'm tired of being treated like one! I do more than you at home!"

Misael was so fired up he was about ready to hop out of his wheelchair just to get to my younger brother.

"Mis, calm down. Ledger, what I tell you about disrespect? What's wrong with you?" My brows dipped, and I brought a hand against my shoulder and took a couple of breaths as Lumi crept up beside me on the little bed while Linc lingered protectively near her.

He was true to form and was his sister's keeper through and through. I feared when she got older and tried to have a life outside of him, Linc was going to lose it. Her chances of having a boyfriend were slim, too, with him around. Sometimes I would just watch them, though. They were so different but the same, if that made sense.

Lumi was usually soft and warm with everyone, a real sweetheart, but if she had a point to prove or felt slighted, watch out. Linc was more reserved. He would shut down in a heartbeat, and when he blew up, it was much like his sister. They rarely fought; it was more like little spats that they could usually work through on their own within a few hours.

"This is some bullshit!" Ledger threw his hands up, pulling me from my dissection of the twins, and marched toward the door, right past Wood, who was watching all my family drama unfold.

"Ledger Omere Grey, you better stop right now and talk to

me!" My reciting his entire government name gave him pause as his hand rested on the door handle. "You are supposed to be my rider, so you better start acting like it!"

"He's been hanging with those little knuckle heads on the street corners," Misael accused, wagging a finger at his grandson. "They all a bunch of thugs with no future."

"At least they got money!" Ledger barked. "It's been helping to feed us when Lishan don't have it!"

My brother's words shattered my heart. I was out there doing all I could, and it still wasn't enough. The thought that he got the inclination to even go out and do God knows what broke me in a way I never expected. He was only twelve years old, and the last thing I ever wanted was for him to become a statistic. I would rather it be me than any of them any day of the week. A single tear slipped past my face, and I laid a kiss on top of Lumi's head.

"Lumi, take Linc and go in the hall with Misael. I need to talk to Ledger." A mixture of melancholy and embarrassment hit me as Wood's dark eyes squinted and studied me.

"Do you mind? What are you even still doing here?" I snapped as Misael wheeled himself toward the door with Linc and Lumi walking ahead of him.

"You can calm all that rah-rah shit down with me. I ain't going nowhere." He folded his arms across his chest and remained at the foot of my bed.

Behind him, Ledger looked on in admiration as he examined him from head to toe in his six-foot stature. Wood was all man, and it was obvious from his stance that he wasn't about any games. He also stayed fly. Even if the nigga was dressed down in sweats and a jersey or some shit, his slides or sneakers always matched, and his jewelry game was ridiculous. He loved wearing a ring on every fucking finger, and not just any ring, rings that were big and gaudy, letting you know he had money.

There were times he was humble and low-key with it, too. Not many saw that side of Wood, though. I appreciated that he could show me that.

"Ledger, come here."

"What?" He stomped past Wood and appeared at my side.

"Don't what me. What is wrong with you? You lying and keeping shit from me?" Still touching my aching shoulder, I closed my eyes and took a breath.

"Like you tell the truth about everything," he called me out, causing Wood to lift a brow as well.

"I do that to protect you. I'm the big sister, remember?" I nudged him. "Get me some water." He reached for the cup Misael poured and reluctantly handed it to me.

"I can help. I been helping. I make runs for Boonie and 'nem—"

"I told you to stay away from them." I clutched the cup and brought it to my lips.

The cool liquid against my lips felt amazing as it traveled down my throat.

"It's making me money! Why you tripping?" he sneered.

I took a breath as I cut my eyes over to Wood. He lowered his arms to his side and rested his hands on the bedrail at the foot of my bed.

"I told you all money ain't good money, Ledger. I do enough of the bullshit to try to keep us afloat. I do the shit, so you don't have to. Now you got me out here taking risks, and you taking risks, which means nobody is at home to look after Lumi and Linc! What happens to them if we both get caught up?"

"I'm tired of being a joke, Lis! Mothafuckas always laughing at us 'cause we ain't got shit! If I can get it, I'm going to." He stomped toward the door.

"Ledger! Where are you going?"

"I'll be around," he said over his shoulder as he ducked out of the room.

I was about ready to hop up and chase after him, but I was connected to too much shit, and Wood was there to stop me. Weakened by just the little movement, my legs dangled over the side of the bed.

"I have to go after him."

"You can't do shit because you just got fucking shot. Lay back and get some rest. I'll take care of this."

"Wood, you don't understand—"

"I understand more than you know, shorty."

"He's my brother. He's all I have. They all are." Tears stung my eyes as he helped me ease back onto the bed.

Resting his fists on either side of me, Wood searched my face before bowing his head. He took a moment before lifting it and searching my desolate stare.

"You could have said something—"

"No. We aren't doing this right now. Find my brother, and then we can talk about it."

Without another word, he bobbed his head. Placing a gentle hand against my collarbone, his oval-shaped coffee bean eyes found mine before he covered my lips in a soft kiss. My eyes shut, taking in the rare affection from him. When I inhaled, it was as if he was pouring life into me. Never had a man tapped into a part of my soul in that way. Instantly, it brought clarity.

"Well, hello there," Yeva greeted us from the doorway as Wood straightened up.

Our eyes locked intensely as he thumbed his bottom lip and faced my cousin. She sized him up, and I immediately caught the thirst in her eyes when she did so.

"'Sup." Wood barely acknowledged her as she moved out of the way so he could leave.

"Whew, shit, is that Wood?" she pried, fanning herself and dramatically throwing her head back.

"That would be him."

"Damn, I see why you ready to risk it all. He is fionnee." She swooned, which brewed jealousy in my heart as she stood near the side of my bed.

"Yeva, what you want?"

"Bitch, be glad I came to check on you. I heard you were shot, and I wanted to make sure you were okay. We are cousins. Where was Ledger going? He was ripping out of here like he was running from something." She pulled up a chair and dropped down into it.

"I'm worried about him. He's getting caught up in these streets, trying to get money."

"He's a boy. It's what they do. He sees you out here doing it, so he figures, why can't he? He's smart, though, and I know you could use the help."

"Yeva, I'm not okay with him out here hugging blocks and possibly getting locked up for it. That shit ain't cool."

"Neither is not having lights or running water," she responded, a little too nonchalant for my liking.

"You can leave. You came and checked on me, and I'm good."

"Oh, so you mad at me for agreeing with the truth?" Yeva sneered. "That's rich. Too bad you aren't. You never will be. Ledger is growing up. How long you think you can keep him in the house, being all domesticated? He's going into those teenage years, and pretty soon, you will be lucky if he's at home at all. As long as he's bringing something to the table, you should be happy."

"That's not what it's about, Yeva."

"Then what is it about, Lishan? From where I sit, you can't do none of this shit by yourself. I commend Ledger for stepping up. That's what he's supposed to do, and you can't fault him for that. He's trying to help lighten your load."

"I don't want him dead or in jail. Do you get that? Or do you just not care?"

"It's all a risk." Yeva shrugged. "It's just about how you do it."

"I couldn't agree with you more." Myra's voice pierced the air, causing me to perk up in my bed and capture her and Merlin coming through the door.

This was the last damn thing I needed while I was trying to recover. Yeva and Merlin exchanged a quick glance. I wasn't sure what that was about as she shifted in her chair, and he came to greet me on the other side of my bed. As far as I knew, they couldn't stand each other, so their brief acknowledgment of one another was noted.

"What's good, Lis? How you feeling?"

"Not like you to be concerned. What can I do for you?" I checked with him and his mother.

"Ma said she talked to you."

"You want to do this now while I'm sitting here in the hospital?" I questioned incredulously as he kissed my cheek, making me cringe.

"You ain't got nothing but time."

"I should get out of here and let you discuss business." Yeva hopped to her feet, and Myra side eyed her. "I am glad you're okay, cuz. We'll talk when you get out of here. I'm here for you, regardless of what you think. I didn't mean anything by any of that. I just know firsthand what you're going through, and I don't see anything wrong with Ledger wanting to help. He's not a kid anymore, and pretty soon, you won't be able to tell him anything anyway."

I let her words register once she was gone. Myra dropped

her bag in the chair my cousin had just vacated and took in my stale hospital room with a turned up nose.

"So, what the hell happened to you?" she asked, popping her gum loudly while raking her questioning eyes all over me.

"Wrong place, wrong time." I shrugged. "What are y'all doing here?"

"Wanted to find out how long you would be recovering. It's time to get to that bag. The other girls are ready. I want to make sure I got all the heavy hitters lined up first. That includes you." Merlin grabbed my hand and gave me a nod.

Slowly, I eased my hand from between his and lowered my gaze to the hospital blanket draped over my legs.

"I can't think about that right now. I almost died, and I got a lot of other shit going on—"

"Make time." Myra gritted her teeth. "We had a deal. I'll give you time to recover, but every day you spend doing that is a day you miss out on making this money."

"Y'all don't give one fuck about me. This is all about money, and right now, my concern is my family."

"You need money to take care of your family," Myra reminded me. "We saw their shoes and clothes, and I know where you live. You just got shot on a job you claim is so good for you. So, tell me, what is the better option right now? You don't have many because I don't see anybody else here trying to take care of you."

Just as the words fell off her lips, the door swung open, and Wylde appeared. My heart relaxed along with the rest of me. I was so relieved to see him. Taking in the energy, his dark eyes went from Myra to Merlin, who was also grilling him, and then to me. His presence was about as powerful as Wood's as he read the room.

"You good?"

"Who the fuck is you?" Merlin growled, locking his jaw as he palmed one of his fists.

Wylde didn't show any fear as the door shut behind him.

"This is my boss." I cleared my throat as Merlin continued to size Wylde up.

Neither he nor Wood were small by any means, so they could be pretty intimidating.

"The fuck he doing here?"

"I need to talk to Lishan. Whatever conversation you got going on is done. Get the fuck out." Wylde flung the door open and nodded.

"Who the fuck—" Merlin was ready to tussle, but Myra snatched up her bag and nodded toward the door. She was smart because the death glare in Wylde's stare hadn't wavered.

"Merlin, let's go. Lishan, we'll be in touch. Very soon." It was more of a warning than a statement.

Merlin's fists were balled at his side as he passed Wylde on his way out the door. He remained unflinching, waiting for the fool to jump since he seemed so confident. With his arms crossed in front of his pelvis, Wylde kept a stoic expression. Merlin looked him up and down one last time before trailing his mama out of my hospital room.

"You saved the day. What's up?"

"What's that about?" He nodded over his shoulder.

"Just some family type shit."

"I came to talk to you about Shayne and what happened." He pulled up a chair and sat at my side.

"I figured. It's all pretty hazy." I squinted and took a breath. "I know we went to the rental property. We were looking around when she got the message from the buyer that they had arrived. Instead of it being the client she thought it was, it turned out to be her baby daddy," I explained.

"Elim," Wylde spoke up with his hands clasped in front of him as his brows came together in anger.

"Yeah, that's what she said."

"So, all that shit she said on the phone—"

"He made her say that. It didn't make any sense because he had shot me anyway. Who was going to believe she went with him willingly after everything he did to her? Shayne lost it when she realized he had the kids, too. She didn't have a choice. When I tried to help fight him with her, that's when he shot me."

"Son of a bitch!" Wylde growled.

"I'm sorry, Wylde."

"It ain't your fault." He shook his head. "I fucked up. Don't worry about anything. There is security posted on your room. There is a hotel with two suites waiting for your grandpa and brothers and sister."

"You don't have to—"

"I didn't." Wylde stood and moved toward the door. "Wood did. He said he would be back with your brother, too. So, don't worry about that. My brother can be hardheaded, shallow, and simple-minded a lot of the time, but one thing he's never lacked is heart. I don't know what happened with y'all, but he told me you were pregnant. Is it his?"

I nodded and looked away.

"I don't know what I'm going to do." I croaked, fighting sudden tears. "I'm damn near a baby myself, and I have more than enough responsibilities."

"You'll figure it out. Take it easy." Wylde let himself out, and I was left unsettled, wrapping my arms around myself in a hug.

Stretching in the bed, I rested my head against the pillow and turned on my side. I was exhausted, and the day was starting to catch up to me. Closing my eyes, I started a prayer not just for myself but for Wood, Ledger, and Shayne. I needed my brother to be okay and not get caught in no bullshit. With Shayne, although I hadn't known her long, I looked up to her, and she was cool. She didn't judge me, and that was rare to find in a female for me. I hoped that she and her kids were safe and that, somehow, she got out of that situation. Drifting off with heavy eyelids, my last thought was of the little seed planted inside me. I prayed for a sign because right now, I didn't have any answers.

"Thought you might need to be reminded who provides for you." Merlin's raspy voice in my ear startled me.

Shifting in the small hospital bed, I tried to reach for my button to call the nurse. His hand was around my throat in a flash, locking down on my vocal cords as he brought his scowling face to mine. Merlin was an attractive man, with full lips and close-set hazel eyes that lit up when he smiled or was humored. Right now, a dark glare also flitted across them as they bounced around mine, and he bit into his bottom lip.

"You tell this nigga, whoever the fuck he is, this shit is dead, you hear me?" He growled, pressing his fingers further into my flesh. "I said, you fucking hear me!" He roared as his warm breath brushed past my face.

I could only nod in response as a wicked grin tugged at the corners of his mouth. My hospital room door burst open, and this big, WrestleMania sized man came charging inside. Snatching Merlin up by the back of his neck, he yanked him with one tug and led him from my bed.

"You shouldn't be in here."

"Get the fuck off me!" Merlin did his best to set himself free, but the guard hemmed him up, lifting both arms above his head and placing him in a headlock. "Lishan, you got me fucked up, bitch! You gon' pay for this!" He kicked his legs like a child, throwing a tantrum as he was dragged toward the door.

With my hand around my throat, I took a couple of deep breaths. I had an entirely new set of problems to deal with when I left this hospital. Merlin wasn't going to rest. He wasn't the type to let shit go. He was also malicious, which meant it wasn't above him to go after Misael or the kids to get to me. I shuddered, thinking about all the evil ways he could come for us. We damn sure weren't safe in the projects. Something had to give.

Unfortunately, we were the only family we had. The rest of them didn't fuck with us. Yeva's mother was dead, and her father had been locked under the jail since she was like six. She was taken into custody by our Uncle Ron, but he turned out to be a pedophile. Yeva ran away when she was fourteen and had been on her own ever since. It made sense why the world had hardened her so much. I didn't want that for my siblings. If I had to die trying, they would have a better life than I had.

Chapter 2
Woodrow Katri

My head was spinning from everything that had taken place in the last few hours. First, we got the call from security at the school that some shit had popped off, and when we got there, Nael was there along with half the damn police force. Apparently, there was some kind of bomb threat or some shit. Amongst all the chaos, Santana and Storm had disappeared. We figured that out when both of their classes had been dismissed and neither of them were present. Nael called Shayne, and we all heard her on speaker. Shit sounded good, but all my alarms were ringing. I knew the shit with Wylde probably put her in a bad headspace, but I didn't believe she would just uproot those kids like that again after everything they had already been through.

Both of the guards we had on Lishan and Shayne had been disabled with a shot to the head. Finding her at the open house fucked me up. I might have been pissed off, but I didn't want shorty to die. The icing on the cake was hearing her tell the nurse she was pregnant when she was being brought in. My stomach and heart had been clenched ever since.

Cruising down the street a couple of blocks from the hospital, I found her little brother, Ledger, trotting along like his ass was on a mission. Little nigga was in need of a haircut and some clothes that fit, but I could tell he had heart. I pulled up beside him and rolled the window down, slowing down so I could keep up with him because he was so mad, he wasn't even paying attention to me.

"Yo, lil' homie, slow up."

"What you doing following me?" A scowl embedded his face when he whirled around, looking just like his damn sister in that moment. Her ass was always looking at a nigga like that.

"Get in the car." I didn't bother glancing his way when I spoke. My tone had enough bass in it for him to figure it out.

I heard him sigh, but he came over and pulled the passenger door open. Once I hit the next corner, I turned the music up full blast. Bobbing my head to some old Scarface, I let the lyrics marinate but kept checking lil' homie out the corner of my eye. We had been driving for at least ten minutes without a word passing between us before I reached over and turned the radio down.

"Why you giving your sister a hard time?" I finally broke the silence.

"I'm not trying to. She don't get it, and you don't either." Ledger shook his head but kept his eyes out his window. "I go to school with kids every day who tease me for being broke and not having parents. Everybody and they mama know that our mama was a hoe who died from aids."

Damn. Shorty really did have it rough. She hadn't shared any of that shit with me. Lishan was so upbeat that I never would have guessed any of this about her life. Now, all the harsh shit I spoke to her was coming back to bite me. I was so hurt that I couldn't see past the shit at the party. She still could have told me, but now that I knew why she was moving how she did, it made more sense.

"How long Lishan been taking care of y'all?" I figured I might as well get all I could out of him since she wasn't forthcoming with the information.

"Since she was thirteen. I was six years old, and the twins were so little. They never even knew our mama."

Swiping my beard, my heart ached, but it wasn't for me. I spent so much time telling myself that shit between me and her was casual that when I started to catch feelings, it pissed me off. I didn't like how she had basically opened a nigga up without my consent and got me to give a damn.

"That punk Merlin and his mama been around ever since. I know he ain't no good, but he has helped. Lishan feels like she owes the nigga or something. So, she goes out at night and dances, he gives her a cut, and she brings it home to take care of us. Our grandpa gets a check, but that goes mainly to all the medicine he has to take since he's so sick. I was trying to get my own money, so she ain't got to worry about me," Ledger broke everything down for me.

"I get that more than you know, kid, but she's your sister. She obviously gives a damn what happens to you."

"I know. I just want to do my part. She shouldn't have to keep doing it all by herself. Merlin don't care either. He just uses her and makes her feel bad. I hate that nigga."

"Aight, tell you what. I'll make sure you and your people straight. I got a homegirl who owns a hair salon and barber shop. I'll hit her up, see if you can come in a couple of times a week and clean for her, get some paper in yo' pocket. What you think about that?"

He seemed to mull over my suggestion.

"What you want in return?" Ledger was smart.

I cracked a smile because he reminded me of myself. He

was wise beyond his years due to his circumstances, and I could already see that he was smart by his word play.

"My sister? The baby she's pregnant with, is it yours?"

"That's between me and her, homie. Looks like we got a lot to talk about."

"Can we stop and grab some food? I'm sure Lumi and Linc are starving. I can grab them a few burgers or something."

"What you want to eat?" I questioned, chucking my chin at him.

"Me? A nice rib platter from the Rib Shack." He tittered, and I bobbed my head.

"Aight, let's go grab some food. I'll hit my homegirl up, and we can go back to the hospital and check on your sister. I already booked a couple of rooms for y'all to stay in tonight. Is there anything else you might need to grab from y'all spot?"

"Misael is going to need his meds. I can go and grab that." Ledger nodded.

"Aight, well sit back then, homie. You ain't gotta worry about shit when you riding with me." I patted his chest.

Ledger adjusted the seat, and I saw a little tension release from him. Traveling through the hood brought me back to a dark childhood. It wasn't all bad, but we damn sure had our share of trauma between our parents. When Wylde and I left all those years ago, we left the city in our rearview. I vowed never to come back there again, and instantly, I was reminded why as we arrived in the projects. There were barely any street-lights lit, and I was rolling with my burner in my lap. Parking on the curb, I glanced up at the building that was in need of some restructuring.

"This where y'all stay?"

"Yeah. I can just go up right quick and get—"

"Nah, I'm coming with you," I insisted, and we piled out together.

I hit the alarm on my shit on our way toward the building on the cracked sidewalk, which was also covered in litter. Just outside the building was a group of young niggas looking like they were waiting to jack somebody or fuck up someone's night. They were all laughing and shit as we approached.

"What's up, Ledger? Nigga, them pants been through it. When you gon' get some fresh gear?" one of the little niggas asked, rocking a pair of Timbs and some crisp feed in braids. His face and hands were already covered in tattoos, and the nigga didn't look a day over fifteen.

"Who this nigga? Is that yo' ride?" the dark as night nigga beside him questioned, squinting as he sized me up.

"Yeah, as a matter of fact, it is. They call me Wood. Once upon a time I ran these very blocks. I blew a couple of bitches backs out in here when the building was up to par. Make sure my ride is in the same condition I leave it in, or we gon' have a problem around here, and this whole block gon' feel it. Feel me?"

"Yeah, aight." The little nigga who first addressed Ledger bobbed his head, but I could see the flicker of resentment behind his eyes.

He didn't like being checked in front of his crew. It was obvious he was the leader, but he didn't have shit on me. I didn't give a fuck if I had been gone ten years, wasn't nobody about to run me off or disrespect me in the same hood I grew up in. If they needed a reminder, we could get to it. I nudged Ledger along, so we could get the shit we needed and get the fuck out of there. My trigger finger was already itching.

After walking through the pissy smelling stairwell, we arrived outside their apartment door, and he dug a key out to let us in. The place was small as fuck. As soon as we entered, we were standing in the kitchen and living room. It was clean, but there was paint chipping, the ceiling was discolored, and there were big water stains from years of leaking. The tile in the kitchen was coming up, and the only table they had was a card table and four little folding chairs. I couldn't believe this was how they were living. I decided right then and there they weren't coming back. Ledger moved around in the back and came back with a bag.

"Should I get some clothes for Linc and Lumi?"

"Nah." I shook my head. "Let's go get this food and take it to the hospital. I'll take care of everything else."

He locked up, even though I don't think they had shit in there worth stealing other than the little TV, and we started down the steps. The little gang in front was gone, but I heard voices and footsteps behind us as we padded toward my car. Glancing over my shoulder, I saw the same three boys from earlier coming up behind us and stopping. Just in front of the building near my car was a black on black Wraith. The chrome detail gleamed in the moonlight as the back door opened and a tall figure climbed out.

"You fucked up now," one of the boys taunted as I went for my burner and hit the fob to unlock my whip.

The tall figure seemed familiar as he approached. Draped in True Religion jeans and a matching logo shirt with a bomber jacket over the look, he squinted as he neared me on the side-walk. Every finger was covered in some big, gaudy ass diamonds—much like mine, and this nigga was licking on a fucking lollipop like a sucka as he skimmed me from head to toe.

"Wood?"

"Dalvin?" I replied, narrowing both eyes and carefully taking him in.

"They don't call me that around here no more. I'm D." He laughed and extended his hand. We dapped each other up, and he glanced at Ledger at my side while his crew backed up.

"This yo' people?" He nodded to him.

"Yeah, something like that. These yours?" I bobbed my head at the little niggas behind me as they muttered amongst each other, talking shit.

"Yeah. My little soldiers. You know how that shit go. I didn't even know you snuck yo' ass back in town." He pulled a tightly rolled wood from behind his ear and sparked it. "You trying to get in around here? I'm usually not open to sharing territory, but we go way back. I thought some new nigga was coming in, trying to make a play. So, I told them I would come through and check some shit while I was in the area."

"Nah, I ain't on that. Just taking care of some other shit. Make sure they know who I am, though, so we don't have no problems around here."

"No doubt. You should come through the club sometime. I own a slice of Prized Package. It's some exclusive type shit. We can catch up. Quiet as it's kept, I'm actually looking for a partner. I want to franchise this shit, and I need a mothafucka with some power and some paper behind 'em," he hinted.

"Bet. I'll slide through one day and we can talk." I peeked at his boys over my shoulder and flashed them all a smile. "Y'all stay dangerous out here. Come on." I urged Ledger toward the car, and we both climbed in.

Dalvin joined his crew on the sidewalk, and I could see him watching me through the tint of my ride.

"Most people be worried about D around here. Him and his boys don't play."

"Neither do I. You ain't got shit to worry about, though. Buckle up."

We made a quick run to Walmart to grab a few essentials for him and the twins. I also made sure to get a few things for their grandpa to make sure he was good as far as clothes for the next few days while I tried to figure some other shit out for them. Once we were done, we grabbed some food and headed back to the hospital. I found the twins curled up in chairs outside Lishan's room, both sleeping as best they could while sitting up, and Misael was beside them, scrolling through his government cell. He peeked his head up at me and Ledger as we approached with food, and I gave my guard on the door a nod.

"Where the hell you been, boy?" their grandpa demanded.

"Chill, Pop, we brought food," Ledger announced, raising the bag in his hand.

Linc and Lumi must have smelled the aroma because slowly they both began to stir and stretch before hopping to their feet.

"I'm starving." Linc yawned.

"Everything good here?" I checked with Bentley, the guard.

"We had a little altercation, but I took care of it."

"What type of altercation?" I questioned, not liking the sound of that. "Is Lis okay?"

"That nigga Merlin popped back up," Misael chimed in. "He was trying to flex and put his hands on her. This one took care of it, though." He bobbed his head to the guard.

My jaw locked as I stepped past him so I could check on Lishan. Shorty was sleeping when I walked in. Standing at her side, I watched her take in slow breaths before I reached out and swept some of her locs from her face. She didn't have any make-up on. I was used to seeing her dolled up, which was cool if that's what she liked, but she didn't need it. Her big brown eyes fluttered open, and when she saw it was me, she popped up anxiously.

"Where's L? Is he okay?"

"He's fine. Out in the hall with everybody else. We came back to check on you. I brought some food. I thought after everyone ate, I could drop them off at the hotel."

"Wood, you don't have to do this. We have a home."

"Yeah. I saw that shit, and I don't think any of y'all should be living like that," I argued and watched the embarrassment flicker in her gaze.

"You went to our place? Why?"

"Ledger wanted to get your grandpa's meds for him."

"Still, we'll be fine. I'll be released and—"

"And what? Hmm? You gon' go back to the fucking projects and take care of all y'all plus a baby?" I prodded.

"I didn't say all that. I don't know what I'm going to do about this baby," she whispered as her eyes fell to the thin hospital blanket cloaking her body.

"Is it mine?" I asked, pulling up a chair and taking a seat.

Her misting eyes met mine, holding me hostage.

"The only thing I do at night is dance, Wood. That's it. Is it a job I can be proud of and brag about like working at Katri? No, but it helps pay bills. So, no, I'm not fucking anyone but you."

"Not even that nigga that keep sniffing around here?" I pried, catching her off guard.

"I have in the past fucked with Merlin, but no. Not recently. So, yes, this is your baby. It doesn't mean I'm having it, though. I have too much other shit to worry about. I can't add a baby to this. Between work, the kids, my grandpa, and school—"

"Wait, you in school too?"

All this time we had been fucking, and I had really been sleeping on shorty. At first, she was just somewhere warm to dip my dick in. Over time, she became the only chick out of the bunch that I could tolerate longer than a fucking hour. She could hold a conversation about some real life shit. I guess now I knew why. She didn't even ask me for shit, which is why I would buy her whatever when we were together.

"It's just online courses, but yes. So, imagine trying to do all that and raise a baby by myself."

"Who said you would be doing it alone?" My question caused her to scoff before shaking her head.

"See, that's what I don't want. Your pity or this sense of obligation. Just because I'm pregnant doesn't mean I need you to take care of me. Me and my family don't need your charity."

"You stubborn as fuck, you know that? And Ion give a fuck what you say, you taking my help and my protection." I played with my beard as the door opened and Ledger walked in with food on a plate that he set in front of Lishan.

"I'm sorry I ran out like that," he apologized. "I just want to help, Lis. You do it all by yourself, and I know it's hard. I hear you crying sometimes at night when you come home."

"I thought you were sleeping." She sniffled a few tears back and blinked rapidly to keep them from falling too. "Ledger, I am an adult. I do all this and make all these sacrifices because that's what I'm supposed to do. I don't want you worrying about that. You're so smart, and I know you are going to be great at whatever you do. I can't stop you from doing what you want. You are growing up on me, and I guess I didn't realize how things were starting to burden you too. I hope you will still talk to me, though, and not block me out when shit is bothering you."

"Wood said he has a friend that can hook me up with a job to make some money a few times a week. He got D and Boonie and 'nem to fall back too. You should have seen how shook they was when they realized D knew him." Ledger offered me a lazy smile. "He's cool. I brought you a plate. Everybody else went to the cafeteria to eat. I'm going to join them. I hope you feel better."

"Thanks." Lis smiled as he embraced her and kissed her forehead like he was the older sibling.

As Ledger trotted to the door, I studied shorty as she reached for the plate and took in the barbecue with baked beans and mac and cheese on the side. She moved some of it around first before lifting her eyes to meet mine.

"Thank you. You really didn't have to—" Her emotional ass was getting ready to start crying.

"Eat your food and get some rest. I'll be back." Leaning over, I planted a soft kiss on her mouth, which she didn't fight, before I moved toward the door.

I damn sure wasn't there to argue. I needed to get with Wylde and figure some shit out, though. Emerging into the hallway, I came across my brother pacing with his cell to his ear. When I approached, he flipped it closed.

"What's the word?"

"I'm hopping a flight," he announced, shoving the phone in his pocket. "They fueling the plane now. I talked to Rich. Between him and Nael, I got something to work with. One of my people put me onto some shit. Word has it that the life insurance on Shayne's people was over half a million. She was the sole beneficiary too. Elim been telling anybody who would listen that this was all her. She set her family up to be killed, so they could cash in. At the last minute, she turned on him and decided to keep the money for herself. Elim just happened to live."

Most of this situation had left me with more fucking questions than answers.

"I know you might not want to hear this..."

"What? That Shayne is some snake ass, money hungry ass bitch? That she sat here and played in our fucking faces? You believe that?" my brother interrogated, swiping his beard. "Even Lishan said she put up a fight with the nigga when he showed up. You think she would do that if she was working with him?"

"I don't know. Maybe. He's still her enemy. Now, more than ever if what the streets say is true. Who's to say she wasn't using us and our influence to protect herself? She would have every reason to put up a fight. Shayne ain't some weak bitch either, and she's smart. Maybe this was a play that she initiated."

Pausing, I couldn't help but wonder about Storm and San, though. I loved those little people, so not being around them again was gon' fuck with me.

"What I do know is... I made the same mistake with Lis. So... if that shit means something, then you need to check it out. For you. I also don't put shit past anybody. I mean, how well do we really know her?"

I could tell Wylde was weighing his options. He had always been a man who thought before moving. Love made you do some impulsive shit, though. It took away the rational and left you with high emotions that made you react instantly. It was exactly what I had done with Lishan because being angry was a hell of a lot easier than being hurt.

"You can't just go by yourself though, Wylde."

"I'm not. You stay here with Lishan. Obviously, she needs you, and you can't leave her unprotected. She's carrying your seed. I don't know what happened, or who this mothafucka Merlin is—"

"I'll deal with that bitch ass nigga," I growled.

I hated him on sight, and I already put word out that I wanted to know everything about the nigga. He wasn't going to be a problem for me or Lishan if I could help it. His fuck ass mama could get it too if the bitch came at me wrong. I just needed things to cool off for a while before I turned the heat up on his ass.

"I know, but you gotta be here to do that. I can handle Kansas City. We got connects there. I ain't tripping."

"Obviously this nigga don't give a fuck about anybody. What if you get there and its exactly what Elim said it is? At the end of the day, he shot Lishan. I ain't never been one to sit back and let anything ride."

"I know. We'll deal with it accordingly. I didn't bring it to Nael because I know that's his niece."

"Talk to him after," I suggested. "And be careful."

We dapped each other up and quickly embraced before he turned on his heel toward the elevator. I could see the stress all over him on this one, and for the first time in a long time, I had some words for the Most High. Wylde had to come back from this. He was all the family I had left other than our father. Lately it seemed even he had drifted, so I needed my brother now more than ever.

This situation hit different on a lot of levels, and I saw that if this didn't work in his favor, my brother was going to turn into a beast. They didn't call him Wylde for no reason. The nigga had really calmed down over the years. I was afraid something might wake up that grim reaper that waited dormant inside him.

Wylde Katri

Four hours later...

When I touched down in Kansas City, the homie Rose picked me up from the airport. Born and bred in Wyandotte County, Kansas, if some shit was shaking in the city, he knew about it. His crew was solid and respected. As soon as I got in his car, he slid me a blunt and a pistol with an extra clip.

"That's just to start you off. I can take you to the safe house. There's a car for you, and here's the address you requested." He slid me a slip of paper.

He knew I didn't do all that texting information shit. We

did our shit like the OGs, face to face. Checking the clip in my gun, I saw that I was fully loaded and brought the Backwood to my lips for a puff. My head was fucked up behind all this, so it damn sure was needed.

"Keep in mind, not a lot of niggas around here fuck with Elim to begin with. He stays on his side, and we all have a mutual respect for one another. Don't mean I like the nigga. I been waiting for him to violate, so I would have an excuse to get at him. His brother, Evan, is always out here being reckless, but he ain't stupid enough to fuck with me or mine," Rose explained. "We got your back."

"I appreciate that." I took another toke of the blunt and bobbed my head. "So, what you know about him and Shayne?"

"Just what the streets say." Rose shrugged. "I don't know either of them personally. It was the good girl, thug nigga story. Shayne was well known thanks to her pops. Miles was cool and serviced anybody. Elim was the nigga most feared. When he got with Shayne, they were inseparable. Anytime you saw him, she wasn't far at any public event. He loved being able to floss her since she was the girl everybody wanted. When he got hit, there was a lot of speculation, especially with everything that went down in the ambush with Miles and his wife. I heard he was jealous and controlling behind closed doors. He claimed Shayne took his kids and ran after she had him hit her parents and that she left him for dead."

"What you think?" I pried, passing the blunt back to him.

"A nigga will say anything to protect his ego, but I won't put shit past these scandalous ass women out here either."

"She lied when she moved to Greenwich. Hid who she was and why she was there. Whole time I been thinking I was protecting her, but what if I was enabling her instead?" I questioned, swiveling my head in his direction.

"I damn sure understand needing some clarity on that."

Rose gripped the steering wheel to his Escalade truck a little tighter as he swung the wheel down a darkened street.

After pulling onto a gravel driveway, he parked and shut the lights off as we both took in the two-story brick home in front of us. We each got out, and Rose dug a key out of his pocket to let us into the dark house. A warm glow filled the entryway after he hit the light switch. The aroma of pine and dust indicated that nobody had been here for a while, not even to clean up.

"I got a couple of the homies coming through, so they can back us up. How you want to move on this?" Rose closed the door, and we remained in the hall.

The space was average sized, with a plant stand in one corner and a full-length mirror beside it. A staircase was straight ahead, l-shaped and curving toward the second floor with a large, dark wood banister holding it up.

"I'm direct. I don't do that hide and seek shit. Just be on standby. The element of surprise will work in my favor because he won't be expecting me." I shot Wood a text to let him know I made it.

I wasn't there for no games, just answers. With everything I had invested in Shayne, I needed to know whether or not it was in vain. I didn't like the uncertainty brewing inside me. I was liable to do something I couldn't take back, and regardless of how things ended with us, her children were innocent in all this. At the end of the day, I cared about them as much as I cared about her. It wasn't their fault they came from some fucked up ass parents.

Once I discussed things with Rose and his crew, they all agreed to back me up. I decided to cool out for the night. It had been an eventful day, and I needed to regroup before I dealt with the situation. In the morning, we were going to move first thing, which left me anxious as I poured myself a tall glass of whiskey and dropped onto the leather sectional in the simply decorated living room. When my phone went off, I glanced at the screen and saw that it was an unsaved number.

"Who is this?" I demanded after swiping the bar to pick up and placing the phone to my ear.

"Kaori," her soft voice responded, which left me less defensive as I sighed.

She was part of the reason I had to know too. Her showing up the way she did shook things between Shayne and me. It wasn't all her fault either because, in the past, I had put Kaori on a pedestal, making her unattainable to even me. She was the first woman I was ever vulnerable with. Our history and her knowing my mother bonded us in a way I didn't share with anyone else. It didn't give her a pass over my entire life, though. She had to learn boundaries.

"How you get this number?" Leaning forward on the couch, I kept the glass in my hand as I lowered my head.

Drowning my sorrows damn sure wasn't going to help, but it made me numb to my problems. Talking to Kaori took me back to a simpler time.

"Waker gave it to me," she answered, referencing my father like he was a friend. I knew they kept in touch, especially after her mama died about three years ago. "Where are you? Are you okay?"

"What you want, K?"

"You act like I'm not entitled to my feelings, Wylde. I love you. You know that, and you know it's never fucking changed. No matter the weather or who you're with or who I'm with. You're a part of me. It never mattered how much time we spent apart or any of that. It was always us against everybody. Did you forget that? All that time with that phony bitch, Billie, fucked your head up?"

I was with her until she started bad mouthing the next.

31

Kaori wasn't perfect by far, but she had heart, and I did love her.

"I'm taking care of some shit. I don't have time to sit and make small talk, reminiscing on a past that we can't get back." I gulped the last of my drink.

"Then let's stop talking about the past. You're right. We are grown now, not little kids. I think we both see the bigger picture in life. Maybe everything that has happened was for a reason, and our time to get it right is now."

Yeah, that shit sounded good, but my head couldn't get with it because my heart was tangled in some other shit. I had to tether whatever the fuck this shit was with Shayne, or I wasn't going to be good to anybody, not even myself. I was never one to be down or broken over a woman, but the thought of not having her in my life was like being robbed of air. Pinching the bridge of my nose, I sighed.

"I gotta go, K."

"Wylde, think about it. I'm still in town for the time being. I could stay, if you want," she hinted.

"Don't make no permanent changes for me. Later."

Once I hung up, I dropped the phone in my lap and reached for the Jack Daniels bottle on the table in front of me. I decided to pour another nightcap, take a shower, and attempt to get a little shut eye.

Morning came quickly. I had the address to the Byer's estate memorized since I had looked at it so much. After a cup of coffee and a blunt, my nerves had calmed somewhat. It was almost eleven am when I arrived outside the gates of the mansion just off Ward Parkway in Missouri. Surprisingly, I was let in with no problems, and the iron gate shut tight behind me as I pulled the Range Rover up the driveway and parked behind a fleet of luxury vehicles. Armed guards walked the property with earpieces and designer suits. I clocked two at the door. Climbing out of the SUV, I adjusted the blazer around me and took measured steps to the front porch.

The front door opened as I reached for the doorbell. Without moving an inch, in a battle of wills, I absorbed her blank, glossed over eyes. She was standing in front of me, but the woman I knew was nowhere in sight.

"What are you doing here?" she queried, seemingly sluggish, but also a little anxious and irritable.

Looking her over, physically, she seemed fine. She was dressed in a simple PUMA jogging suit with matching slides. Her hair fell past her shoulders, crowning her bare face.

"The fuck you mean? What the fuck are you doing here?" I rebutted, face hardening into a sneer.

"It's over, Wylde. What else is there to say?" She was speaking, but it didn't sound like Shayne. "I made it pretty clear that I didn't want to be a burden to anyone."

"So, you come back to a mothafucka who hurt you and your entire fucking family? Make that shit make sense. Or, is what they say about you true?"

"And what's that? Hmm? What the fuck they saying about me, Wylde? Please enlighten me!" Her eyes narrowed while piercing me accusingly.

"You a snake. The kind of bitch that will turn on her own people for a dollar. The kind that would put her own children at risk—"

"You can go to hell!" Emotion flickered behind her glare, giving me some sign that the woman I thought I knew was still in there somewhere.

"Tell me I'm wrong."

"I'm not telling you shit! You believe whatever the fuck you want. I did what I had to do for me and my kids," she declared, spearing me with a resentful glare.

"We got a problem here, ma?" Elim's smug ass slid up behind her, dropping a hand to her waist.

Shorty flinched, but it was such a short reaction that you had to be looking for it. She didn't resist him, though, as he carefully assessed me on his doorstep.

"No. Not at all."

"I understand the effort." Elim licked his lips and kissed the side of Shayne's face. "But you need to leave. She made her choice, and it ain't you. What you failed to realize is, me and Shayne got history. I'm sure you know all about it. You had other bitches before her. Sometimes it's hard to break those connections. You start missing that old thang." He tittered nostalgically while glancing at her.

It was like knowing two different people. The woman in front of me didn't resemble who I had spent time with. The fact that she could play the role so fluidly was mind-blowing. This version of her was hard, damn near ice cold, and callous as fuck.

"Now, I must not be as bad as she says if she's here with me, right? The truth is, we both a little toxic. Ain't that right, baby mama?" Elim angled his head, so it was practically resting against hers.

I noticed he kept his hand near his waistband, trained to go, but I wasn't here for that unless provoked. Rose and his crew were simply a precaution. All I wanted was answers, so I wasn't dumb enough to come here on some street shit. Whether Shayne was in the picture or not, for what he did to Lishan, he was going to pay. It wasn't on me. My brother was a hothead behind bullshit some days, so just imagine if you fucked with something he was truly starting to care about. Shayne made the decision to switch sides, but I couldn't say that would hold her exempt from him too when he found out.

"That's how you want it?" My question was for her, so that's who I was focused on.

This fuck nigga didn't scare me. I just had to be sure before war was declared. One thing I learned from Rich was you looked your enemy in the eye before striking. I respected a mothafucka as long as they gave it back. Elim had little regard for life, and that was always dangerous in any human being.

"Tell this nigga what it is, so he can get the fuck off my property." Elim flicked the tip of his nose, clearly losing patience.

"Goodbye, Wylde. Ain't nothing for you here. I'm exactly where I'm supposed to be." Her tone remained even, void of any emotion, fucking robotic as her eyes bore into mine without so much as a blink.

"You heard her." A gleam of satisfaction broke out across Elim's face beside her.

"And you hear me." This time, I spun to him, keeping her separate from the conversation. "You might think you got away with something, but you didn't. See, that girl you shot, she's still very much alive." From my peripheral, I peeped the resolve in Shayne's face as she finally let a relieved breath escape. "She also means something to my brother, and he's not the type to let things go. I can't control him when he gets something in his head..." I emphasized with a gesture to my temple while remaining completely collected.

"Then you might want to start picking a plot now. I don't take to threats."

"Neither do we. So, enjoy life while you can. You never know when everything will change." Forcing a tight grin across my face, I examined Shayne's taut posture and the way Elim held her in place against him.

If this was what she wanted, I wasn't one to stand in the way.

She had told me everything I needed to hear. I was never a begging type, and I damn sure wasn't about to start now. Giving her one last glance, I shook my head and backed away from the door. Once I got in the car, I took one final glimpse of the house and started the engine. The turmoil boiling was beginning to simmer, but something still lingered. No lie, a nigga had been gutted. I was hollow now, even more than before. For a split second, I wondered if all the bitches' hearts I'd hurt had felt like this. I couldn't dwell on it for too long. The door closed, and for me, so did this chapter of my fucking life. Not everything was meant to last.

Chapter 3
Shayne Rogan

About five weeks later...

My days were all running together. Some were long, others short. When pills weren't being forced down my throat, or I wasn't being injected with something, I was too drained of energy to do anything else. At first, Elim kept me in that state to subdue me, making me put up less of a fight. When it came to him touching me, I needed to be outside of myself, so I accepted it. It was the only way I was able to get through him being on top of me, kissing me, and invading the space between my legs. I had a little hope when Wylde arrived that I would be rescued, but Elim was smarter than that. If nothing else, he knew how to manipulate some shit.

For years, he had been spinning false tales of what happened to suit his own reputation. I always said the nigga's ego was more bruised than anything during all this. The way he was holding me hostage like something he possessed told me everything I needed to know.

The main concern I had was keeping it together for Santana and Storm. I knew I had to get out of here, though, and that we were on our own. Wylde was questioning me, and I shouldn't have been mad because Elim did have me looking like some scheming ass bitch to the rest of the world, but I wanted Wylde to know better off the strength of us. Maybe I had gotten caught up too fast with him. Obviously, we weren't as bonded as I thought. Since he made it clear that he wasn't coming to my rescue, and Elim had threatened to kill him in front of me if he did, I knew the only person I could count on was me to break away. I didn't care how long it took or what I had to do.

Elim's mom, Caterina, made it a point to keep me separated from Storm and San. I saw them during meals most of the time. As far as I knew, they were in one wing of the house, and I was held captive in another. It was better for them to see as little of me in that state as possible. I wasn't their mother. I couldn't do anything for either of them until I knew I could get out of here with them. Every day, I was screaming in my own head to get my shit together and figure a way out of this, but I won't lie, sometimes I let the drugs take over. On those days, Elim was almost tolerable.

"Good morning, baby." He pressed his lips against my cheek, draping an arm over my stomach beside me in bed.

Lately, waking up to him made me sick in the literal and metaphorical sense. My stomach flipped anxiously as his morning wood stretched along my thigh. I was still fuzzy in the head from the day prior. His touch did nothing for me, and I hated always being sluggish. Groaning, I shifted away from him so I could shower and handle my hygiene. I was given time on the grounds to walk, as long as there was a guard nearby, and I looked forward to those outings. The warm sun on my face reminded me that I wasn't dead. I just had to figure a way out of this mess. It was easier said than done when I had five sets of eyes on me every single day. I felt like I was under a damn microscope.

"Where you going?" He pinned me to the mattress and draped his heavy body over mine. His lips traced kisses along my neck and up to my cheek before finally capturing mine. I had to force myself to kiss him back.

"Elim, I feel... sick." I jumped up, and he slid off to the side as I raced to the bathroom just steps from the bed we slept in.

Throwing myself over the toilet, I tossed up the contents of dinner last night and dry heaved until I was on E. Using the back of my hand, I wiped my mouth and flushed the toilet before slowly approaching the mirror above the sink.

"The fuck wrong with you?" From the doorway he peered in at me with his face all balled up. "Every time I get close to you now, all of a sudden, you sick."

"Maybe it's all the fucking drugs you're pumping into me," I acknowledged and reached for my toothbrush.

Nowadays, I wasn't right if I wasn't high. On top of all the other shit, the nigga had also made me an addict. Pills were my drug of choice if I wasn't smoking weed or drinking. He had turned me out, and since I didn't do shit else with my days, I was on a twenty-four-hour ride, only coming down to sleep.

"So, you blaming me?"

"No," I quickly rebutted as I squeezed toothpaste onto my brush. "I'm sorry. I didn't mean that." I knew if I didn't clean that shit up, it would turn into yet another battle, which I didn't need.

He swiped his hand down his face and let go of a sigh before stepping up in the mirror behind me. Hugging me in his tatted arms, he brought me against his solid body.

"Why don't we do something together? You, me, and the kids. We can get out of here for a few hours, hit the amusement park or something. I know you been here, and you haven't felt like you've had much freedom."

"Because I haven't," I muttered, brushing my teeth and ignoring him as he continued to osculate my neck.

His touch had my skin crawling, but there was nothing I could do about it. For the first two weeks, I fought him on every single thing, even while I was drugged, but he was pumping me full of so many narcotics that it became inevitable that he would have his way with me. Most of the time, I barely remembered and couldn't feel a thing. A lot of times, I pictured Wylde instead of him, and that helped me get through it. I wasn't sure how long it had been, but it seemed like so long ago since I had last been with him. I missed his touch, the way he held me so close when we finished making love, like he never wanted to let me go. Staying high became an escape in more ways than one.

I knew it was more of a mental game with Elim, and I had to bide my time. The hardest part was faking it. I should have been used to it since I had done it for the last ten years, but after being handled by somebody like Wylde, it was more challenging than I thought. Elim was so far removed from what I desired in a man now, and he couldn't see that past his own ego.

Getting him away from his family was going to be the first item on my agenda. With Caterina constantly in his ear, he was never going to be a man. His father was of no help since he was barely around to even grasp what was going on. He played indifferent to everything, and it was more than likely so he could keep his own dirt off his wife's radar. She seemed far more interested in what she could control, anyway, which was her children and household.

"So, get dressed. I will have Ma get the kids ready. We can go shopping and shit. You used to love when I took you on shopping sprees. Plus, it looks good for the reporters and shit to see us out doing normal things. The engagement announcement just hit."

Shaking away the disheartening thoughts as best as I could, I ran a shower so I could get fresh as Elim pulled away from me to go handle some business. The engagement came out of left field. We were together for ten years, and the nigga always shied away from the topic of marriage. Now, suddenly, he couldn't wait to make shit official. I believed he just had a point to prove. The rumors about our relationship had been swirling for years, and most of them made him appear weak. Even now, he was acting out of pure ego. Locking me down and showing everyone how he dominated me was his only goal.

We slept in the same room, but the nigga was like a covert spy or some shit. He didn't keep his phone in the bedroom, and he locked us inside it every night. On days when he went off to work, I was usually held up in here until Caterina decided to have someone on the staff come serve me something to eat. Leaving it up to her, she would let me starve. I didn't all the way trust her serving me anything anyway. Since I had been there, we hadn't shared many words. I just hated that she was the influence over my children. I missed them so much. I hated that Elim was able to snatch us so easily out of the life that we were building.

Once I showered and cleansed myself with the Hermes body wash that I loved, I slid a towel around my damp frame and studied myself in the mirror. I could tell that I was stressed, but my weight hadn't completely plummeted, which I was glad for. Ironically, I still had an appetite as of late; it was just certain things that triggered my nausea. Desolation reflected in my eyes. I didn't see any life staring back at me through them. After dressing casually in a pair of distressed stone washed jeans, an ivory top, and a plaid cardigan that hung to my calves in different shades of brown, tan, and burnt orange, I took one last glance at myself in the mirror.

One thing was for certain, Elim knew how to spoil. He was just terrible at everything else. It would all be so simple to live here and play content, but I knew I no longer wanted to move through life settling for a damn thing. I could have every luxury with him, and I still wouldn't be happy. Admiring my wavy curls, I noted that my bob was in need of a trim because it was well past my shoulders now. After I applied a coat of Fenty gloss to my lips, I went to slip into my wheat Timbs.

"Damn, you look good," Elim complimented once he unlocked the door and let himself back inside. "You ready? I thought we could have breakfast first."

"Yeah. Let me grab my purse." I shuffled over to a nearby chair and grabbed the Fendi bag.

After slinging an arm over my shoulder, he led me down the stairs to the kitchen. I was still so drained, but seeing Storm and Santana at the table immediately brightened my day. Each of them cut dismal eyes in my direction, breaking my heart. Usually, I would get a smile, and they would be jumping up and down to see me, even when I was too out of it to have a genuine reaction. Something had changed.

"Well, good morning." Caterina stood at the stove, stirring something in a pot.

Every time she saw me, she turned her nose up, and a cold glare rested behind her stare. With an apron tied around her waist, smoking a cigarette, she blew a cloud in my direction and looked me up and down. It was obvious that she was against me being there every time she laid eyes on me.

"The kids ready to go?"

"As soon as they finish eating. I told them if they don't clear those plates, they won't be going anywhere. I don't know what kind of parenting she's been doing, but it's obvious they need a few lessons in respect. Don't worry, I'll take care of that." She turned the burner off on the stove and strolled over to the counter to grab a glass.

It wasn't 10:00 a.m., and this woman was drinking hard liquor. After taking a gulp, she strolled over to the table where my babies were seated and stood between them. Her gaze traveled from Storm to Santana and examined their plates.

"Santana, go get your shoes. Storm, you will be staying here unless you finish that fruit."

"I don't like bananas!" Storm screamed.

The swift smack Caterina sent to her face rocked my entire body, sending a complete shockwave through it. Within seconds, I was on her as Storm's little body fell out of her chair. My daughter hit the floor and burst into tears with a hand against her face.

"Don't you ever touch her again!" I swung on Caterina, but Elim was there to snatch me up before I could lay a finger on her.

"Bitch, who the fuck you think you talking to?" She flicked her cigarette at me as Elim propped himself between us.

"Ma—"

"I told you what to do with this bitch!" She aimed her long, overly decorated acrylic nail on her index finger at me. "She don't belong here, and if she disrespects me in my fucking house again—"

"The fuck you gon' do." I coughed up enough spit so when I stepped forward, a nice wad flew out of my mouth and against her chest.

"No this hoe didn't!" Charging forward, her abrupt movements sent Elim flying to the side, and she snatched me up by a fistful of my hair.

I swung on her so hard that when it connected with her jaw, it released her hold on me, and she stumbled toward the large oak table. Santana had to jump up from his chair to avoid that bitch falling over him. He ducked into a corner as Storm took off out of the kitchen. I was easily winded since I hadn't been at my strongest the last few weeks, so she was able to gain an upper hand and rush me into the island counter a few feet away.

Her fist collided into my face a couple of times, throwing me off my square before I reached for a nearby plate and brought that shit down on her head. It was enough to get her to back off, and I lifted my leg to kick her to her shiny marble floors. She struggled to get on her feet, and Elim spun on me with a smack so hard to my face that I staggered into one of the bar chairs. The warm liquid running down my upper lip and the sudden metallic taste on my tongue let me know he had drawn blood. My eyes fell on the counter, and I instantly reached for the butcher knife left on top of a cutting board.

"You better think about what the fuck you doing, ma," Elim warned in a low growl.

With the sharp edge pointed at him, I raised my chin.

"The fuck I got to lose?"

"Handle this bitch, Elim, or I will!" His mother wiped the blood from the corner of her mouth and reached up to check the cut on her forehead that was also leaking. Panting and practically foaming at the mouth, she tried to get at me again.

"Where's Storm?" I asked, eyes darting around the room.

"About to get her ass beat, right along with you!" Caterina rushed off, and Elim focused on me.

"Be smart here, ma. This ain't gon' end well for you. You really want me to do this in front of the kid?" Elim nodded over his shoulder to Santana, hiding in the pantry and poking his head just beyond the frame of the door.

The fear I saw in his misting eyes sliced my heart open. I promised myself I would never allow them to witness anything like this again. Tears welled while my hand trembled. Elim moved in when he witnessed me weakening. Snatching the knife from my hand, he pinned me against the counter and brought it to my throat. With his mouth clenched tight, his face came so close it was nearly touching mine as his wild eyes deadlocked on me.

"That's what the fuck I thought. That was some disrespectful shit you just did! You gon' pay with yo' fucking freedom. I thought we could spend the day trying to put our shit back together—"

"Fuck you!" I spat. "I fucking hate you! You took everything from me, and I would rather walk through glass and burn in hell than ever be with you again! Every time you touch me, I want to fucking kill myself!" The jig was up.

Him and that bitch ass mama of his had woken a beast, and I wasn't going down without a fight. His fist struck my face, and Santana ran up on his father swinging. It caught Elim off guard as I crumbled at his feet, and he spun so he could snatch our son up.

"Little nigga, the fuck wrong with you?" he barked, holding San in the air with his feet dangling as he stretched his shirt.

"Keep yo' hands off my mama!" He was still trying to land a punch as Elim tossed him onto the floor.

Our son didn't budge as his father hovered over him, his carbon black orbs bathed in shadows. His little chest heaved as he prepared himself for Elim's wrath.

"This my bitch!" Elim pointed an index finger at me. "And you came from my nut sack. I'm yo' fuckin' father! If you ever run up on me like that again, you gon' get schooled on respect, son! We clear?" Elim threatened, resting a hand on his hip where his pistol rested. "I asked you a fucking question!" Drawing his gun, he kept it at his side to emphasize his point, and Santana slowly bobbed his head.

"Let me go!" Storm was screaming and throwing an entire fit as Caterina dragged her back into the kitchen by her thick crown of hair. I had never seen her act out like that before, and Caterina didn't care that she was hurting her.

"Ma, the fuck you doing?" Elim sneered and tucked his gun.

"I found her in my office with my cell phone." She held her phone up. "She made a call to someone."

The amount of pride in my chest for Storm in that moment was overwhelming.

"I hate it here! I want to go home! I don't like you!" My baby girl was going off, little arms flailing in an attempt to connect her fists to her grandmother and everything.

Elim rushed to grab her and scooped her into his arms. Flipping her around he used the palm of his hand to whup her until she was wailing and too weak to put up a fight. When I tried to get to her, his mama stepped in front of me with evil blanketing her stare.

"I warned you. I told Elim that you were trouble from day one. He should have left you at that fucking garage where he found you." Her lips curved into a sullied grin.

She popped the cap off a syringe and brought it to my arm before I could even protest. After the needle was jammed into my flesh, I instantly grew dizzy, weak, and nauseous as hell before I collapsed at her feet. The room tilted, and my gaze latched onto Santana's as he curled up on the floor not far away. I wanted to say something or reach for him, but my body was shutting down.

Wylde Katri

"Mmm..." Kaori moaned, twerking on the dick as her box juiced up and released like a waterfall.

There was no denying shorty and her A1 pussy. She damn sure could make you forget your troubles. Being with her again reminded me of us getting together as kids. The shit was kind of nostalgic, taking me back to a time when my mama was also alive and banking on us spending our life together. As soon as my nut dropped, any desire I had for her did as well, though. I was already knocking through her walls with images of Shayne floating through my head.

No matter what I did to flush shorty out, nothing seemed to fucking help. I was still trying to come to terms with how she came into my life and shook everything up in such a short amount of time. For the last month, Kaori had been lingering around. When she found out Shayne was out of the picture, I guess it gave her some incentive. I wasn't supposed to fall into shit with her, but my head was fucked up about my girl, and it was easier to drown my sorrows in alcohol and my dick deep in some pussy than to talk or think about the situation that was out of my control.

"Damn, Wylde. You are tense, baby." She reached down to rub my shoulders, but I nudged her off me, so I could go take a shower.

After that round, I was in need of some cleansing. At this point, I was going through the motions. Once I brushed my teeth and took care of the rest of my hygiene, I slipped into black jeans, a gray sweater, my all black Prada boots, and threw on a black peacoat as I snatched my keys, phone, and wallet from the dresser. The full brunt of winter had hit, so we were layering up around these parts.

"Where are you going?" Kaori frowned as she slid to the foot of the bed.

"I got some business to take care of. Lock up when you leave." My movements toward the door alarmed her, and she jumped up, still tangled in the sheets while reaching for my arm.

"What's going on with you?"

"You got what you came here for, K. The fuck else you want?" Violently yanking away from her sent her flinching in alarm.

"What exactly did you think I came here for, Wylde? What is wrong with you? All I've been doing is trying to connect with you, and all you keep doing is pulling away," she accused as her face fell into a pout.

"I ain't got time for this shit. I gotta go."

"Are you still in your feelings about that baby mama bitch?" she sneered, and my hand froze on the knob to my bedroom door.

Shayne might not have been around, but she was still a trigger for a nigga, and listening to Kaori talk about her like that only fed my rage. I was liable to snatch her fucking head off. So, instead of responding, I stormed out of the room. I was back at the house Wood and I were sharing, but I spent my time in the basement where there was a private entrance and a bathroom and kitchen. Shit was like my own apartment. With Lishan and her family there, I pretty much went to work, the gym, and stayed out the way.

Wood had stepped into the role of provider for Lishan and her entire family. It wasn't shit for him to go to the grocery store or bring home dinner. The nigga spent most nights helping the twins with homework and playing games on the PS5 with Ledger. I couldn't be mad at it. I moved just as quickly with Shayne. The house wasn't necessarily crowded since everyone pretty much had their own space. I hadn't planned to make it permanent, though. I just hadn't taken the time to decide my next move yet. Greenwich was home, and I wasn't leaving any time soon, so I wanted my next place to be something custom for me.

Staying at Shayne's place wasn't an option, even though a lot of my shit was there. Being in that space without her or the kids was why I refused to go there. It was too much. Nael was still holding out hope that she would come home, and something else seemed to have him preoccupied, so I wasn't tripping. I imagined he needed to process some shit just like the rest of us. The house was paid for anyway, so it didn't matter what we did with it. I just knew I wasn't moving in.

Surprisingly, I found Wood in the kitchen, stuffing his face with Lucky Charms at the waist high island. He was fully dressed in denim and a navy Polo t-shirt with his navy and gold Vapormax on his feet. His platinum and diamond Cuban link draped over his neck, and on his middle finger was his favorite gaudy diamond that resembled a Superbowl ring. Clearly, he woke up ready for anything. I went to brew myself a cup of coffee as he hovered over his bowl with his head down.

"What you doing in here looking all thoughtful for?" I questioned, grabbing a medium roast pod and sticking it in the Keurig.

"I just needed a minute." Wood muttered, moving his spoon around in his bowl. "Shit is heavy with Lishan. I ain't equipped for that emotional shit. She pregnant on top of everything else. I did what I could, giving them a place to stay, and she even fighting me on that. The fuck I'm supposed to do?"

"You know what it's time to do." I folded my arms across my chest. "Wake they shit up. Mothafuckas had time to settle in, get comfortable, and think shit sweet."

"We talking about my situation or yours?" Leaving his spoon in his bowl, he reclined in his chair. "Look what made the news." He tossed a newspaper article in my face and shot a quick glance in my direction.

There was a full photo of an engagement announcement with Shayne and her ex's face. A brief article covered one side of the page, giving a glimpse of the couple's life together. It detailed how long they had been together, their children, and a bunch of other miscellaneous shit about Elim's family, painting a perfect picture. He was beaming proudly, with an arm draped around her waist as a tight smile curved her mouth. Her gaze was void. I was always told the windows to the soul were the eyes, and Shayne's were empty, downcast. She was out of place beside him, but the diamond on her finger told another story.

"The fuck is this?" I tossed the paper back at him.

"Reality," Wood responded. "You sitting around here kicking yourself when she went back willingly to a situation that nearly broke her. I wanted to give her the benefit of the doubt too, but this... the fuck is this? It's been over a month. She let that nigga get back in her head. Me, you, and even Nael need to accept that." His cell started to ring, vibrating against the countertop as he frowned at the display.

The number wasn't saved, but Wood wasn't big on storing people anyway unless he dealt with you regularly. When he picked up, he immediately put the phone on speaker.

"Who the fuck is this?"

"Uncle Wood." The soft whimper on the other side of the phone sent his eyes popping up and syncing with mine.

"Storm?" he checked, picking the phone up and examining the screen. "What's wrong, lil mama?"

"The mean lady hit me. I don't like it here. I want to come home." Her little cries sent rage into my brother's eyes as his hand tightened around his device.

The throbbing of my heart in my chest had me ready to blow the fuck up as my head filled with dark thoughts. The fear in her voice angered me.

"Where you at? Tell me," he prompted, but the shouting and screams in the background overpowered her words.

Storm must have been hiding or something because I heard a creak like a door opened and then scuffling of feet before the phone dropped, and there was more movement. Her high pitched screams gutted me as someone picked up and started to breathe on the line.

"Who the hell is this?" The cold, raspy voice of a woman could be heard while the screaming and ranting in the background continued.

I could have sworn I heard Shayne's elevated voice.

"If you hurt that little girl, it's the last mothafucka's face you gon' see, bitch!" Wood threatened before the line went dead.

"What's the area code for that number?" I asked, pausing at the counter.

"816."

Kansas City.

"What you thinking?"

Studying the image in the paper, I couldn't be sure what was what as I started putting pieces together of an imaginary puzzle in my head. Something was damn sure off about this whole shit. I didn't give a fuck about this supposed announcement. All my alarms were ringing. I might have fucked up with Shayne and misjudged the situation. I knew she was hurt by seeing me with Kaori, and I knew Elim was a bitch nigga who would do anything to break her down. I couldn't wrap my mind around her suddenly leaving to be with a nigga like that again, though. I did my research on him and his family, and they were about as connected and influential as mine.

The doors I was able to knock down were tight lipped when it came to the Byers name, which meant their reach went beyond what I thought. As much as I told myself I was letting it go, something wouldn't let me. Since I met this girl, I had been moving off pure instinct. It was how I knew to be there that first night he sent his goons after her.

"Call Rose. Tell him to get his people ready."

Wood picked his phone up and started the phone tree to our squad. I told him I had something to handle and left him to get packed while I took a quick drive. It wasn't often that I decided to check on Nael. Like I said, being in that house just wasn't the same. At one point, it almost seemed like home, but now it was hollow and full of *what ifs*. I parked in the curved driveway and sat there, running back all the simple moments that had already been planted in my mind before approaching the door. I had faced another blunt on the drive, but even that wouldn't settle my mind. When I reached the door after minutes of sitting in my car, going back and forth, Nael propped it open before I could even raise a hand to knock.

"You hear anything?"

"Wood got a call. We're going to Kansas City."

My firm gaze met with his. His hooded orbs narrowed as they turned into slits of scrutiny. Nael stepped aside and let me into the foyer.

"It's a risk, going against that family. Many have tried." He stroked his beard while his intuitive eyes pierced me.

"Tried and failed. I got resources too. I'm taking every precaution. And me and my team don't lose. I don't know what Shayne is on. I just know something ain't right, and if nothing else, we have to get San and Storm out of there."

"You're right, and I'm coming with you." Nael nodded in complete agreement.

"Okay, Pack a bag. Our plane should be ready to go, and if anything, I know that Storm and San are going to need you."

Elim

"How many times have I told you, Elim? How many times you gon' fall victim to this bitch?" Ma blew smoke from her lungs as she remained seated at the counter with her glass in front of her.

A few hours had passed, and I was still going back and forth in my head on how to deal with Shayne. Tossing back a shot of tequila, I glared across the countertop. I wasn't in the mood for this shit. When I woke up this morning, I was trying to actively put my life back together, and Shayne had single-handedly fucked that up. She was becoming more of a problem, and I was starting to think my mama was right.

"I don't want to hear this shit right now, Ma." Smacking my lips, I snatched the bottle up.

"Obviously, you need to hear it after the shit that went down here today. You need to get your children under control and take care of that bitch once and for all. She made it clear that she doesn't want you. She don't even respect you. You holding onto hope, trying to control her, and all you're doing is keeping an enemy close." She gulped her gin and took another drag from her cigarette. "Take care of her, or I will."

Once I had a couple more shots, I went for my gun in my waist and marched toward the door to our soundproof basement. I took the stairs slowly as it shut behind me. I didn't want any of this, but she had pushed me too far. I wondered if her or these fucking kids were even worth it. The disrespect had me so keyed up that it was causing me to rethink everything.

Approaching the door, I took a breath and dug the key out of my pocket to unlock it. I heard the whimpering before turning and seeing that Storm and Santana were in a corner huddled up together, with Shayne lying on her side in the middle of the floor.

"See what y'all made me do?" I queried, looking between both kids as they held onto each other. "Let this be a lesson to you. From now on, you do what I say. You understand me?" I was met with silence, which only infuriated me more. "I said, do you fucking understand me!"

"Yes." Santana's voice was strong as he kept an arm draped over Storm's shoulder and shot daggers at me like I was some random mothafucka off the street and not his father.

"Elim!" My mother hissed down the steps.

"I'm handling shit, Ma—"

"We got company. Bring those kids up here and lock that door," Ma instructed.

Shayne was a liability I didn't need. I couldn't count on her to be my other half. She didn't trust me any more than I trusted her. I wanted my children close, but our relationship was already fractured thanks to her. Moms was right, she had to go. With Shayne no longer in the picture, there wasn't that type of influence over them. She would teach them to disrespect and resent me, and I couldn't let that happen. My kids were all I had left, and I'd be damned if anyone turned them against me.

"Let's go," I urged, waving the gun as they scrambled to their feet.

I let them start up the steps first and made sure to keep Shayne secured in the room before locking up and trailing them up the staircase.

"The fuck is going on?" I asked, noticing the stricken expression on my mother's face before darkness swirled in her eyes, and she fixed them on Storm.

"Who did you call, little girl?"

"Who the fuck is here?"

"Some bitch and a damn cop," Ma answered, cutting a hard glare in both of my children's faces. "You both better be on your best behavior. You say anything wrong, and that's your ass, and you won't ever see your mama again," she warned. "Go make sure your rooms are clean too." She snapped her fingers and rushed them along.

Ma fixed her hair in the mirror near the door and adjusted the pantsuit she wore before putting her cigarette out in an ashtray.

"Get your shit together, Elim." She ordered, giving me that look she always had since I was a child.

I smoothed out my shirt and gulped the rest of my liquor before tucking the glass in a drawer and putting my pistol behind my back. When she flung the door open, the cool air hit us first, and my dick sprang to attention at the baddie in the doorway. Shit! If I didn't have enough women problems, I would damn sure throw her tender ass in rotation. She rocked a short bob with a slight bang, and her eyes were slanted upward as they examined my mother first, and then me. In a gray and black pinstriped suit, her arms remained crossed behind her back.

"May I help you?" Ma questioned, hand on her hip and full of attitude.

"Sarah Reeves with the Department for Children and Families," she introduced, quickly flashing her badge in my mother's face. "This is officer Duncan. We received a child welfare check call. May we come in, please?"

"What kind of welfare check?" Ma sneered.

"Are there children in this house?" Sarah questioned.

"My children," I told her, calmly stepping forward and admiring her smooth, tan skin and full, juicy lips that were tinted with an orange red color that complemented her skin. "Storm, Santana, get down here!" I barked up the nearby staircase.

Their slow steps grew closer as they reached the top and began to come down slowly together. Although physically they appeared fine, there was something in their eyes that was striking, and anyone would question it. Ma moved aside so Sarah could enter with the officer. He was about six feet tall and almost two hundred pounds. I caught the tattoos on his hands as he clasped them together in front of him. He was in uniform, and everything appeared legit, but I didn't like how he was giving himself a tour of the entryway, checking past the doorways into the many rooms of my parents' mansion.

"Hi, there." Sarah's gaze softened on my kids as a small smile broke out across her lips. "My name is Sarah. What's yours?"

"Storm," my little girl whispered as her eyes fell on the ground.

With her hair in two goddess braids, she was adorable, but her face was flushed, and her tone somber.

"Nice to meet you, Storm. And you are?" She turned to San next, and he stuck his chest out before chucking his chin.

I had to half smile because the little nigga had heart. I would have to break that against me, though. Being with Shayne had made him soft on certain shit, and I couldn't have my son being all empathetic. My father always taught me that I had to rule with an iron fist over these women. Santana was going to be brought up the same way. A woman had a position to play, and if she didn't like it, you made it clear she didn't have any other option.

"Santana."

"Well, it's nice to meet you. Everything okay here? We got a call that there might be some sort of domestic situation, and our priority is making sure that these children are safe. Is your wife here?" Sarah spun to me, and my face crinkled in confusion.

"My wife?" I repeated, looking past her at my mother. "Oh,

you mean my baby mama? Yeah, she's not here. We got into a little dispute over some wedding shit, and she took off."

Sarah scrutinized me carefully. I could tell she didn't believe me, but what the fuck was she going to do, search the house? She didn't have any real grounds for that. The officer was there as a precaution. She half turned, exchanging a glance with him before he nodded. Lifting her brows, Sarah bowed her head.

"Everything seems fine here. Thank you for your time."

Once they were gone, Ma slammed the door hard before searing me with a laser stare like I had summoned them. She went to grab her pack of cigarettes and dug one out of the box. Her dark eyes landed on San and Storm as they cowered near the stairs, now that the social worker and officer had left.

"You two are lucky." With the Newport between her middle and index finger, she signaled to them. "Don't think anybody is coming to save you. This is your family, so you better start acting like it. All that shit your mama taught you is done!" She made a slicing motion against her throat. "You are Byers children! That's how you're going to be raised, and you will follow the rules around here. Are we clear?" she questioned, tight eyes bouncing from Storm's frightened face to Santana's hard glare.

He was doing his best to stay tough.

"I said are we fucking clear!" Ma screeched, making them both jolt in terror. "You say, yes ma'am."

"Yes, ma'am," they recited in unison.

"Now, go upstairs and make sure those rooms are clean. I'll deal with you two later." She shooed them off. "Tonight, you take care of that bitch, Elim. We are done with this. Those kids are better off without her, and so are you."

I couldn't agree more. I had given this shit with Shayne too much attention. It was time to move on with my life, and my kids would have to adjust to not having a mother. The gloves had come off, and she had shown me that she was never going to be down. I would spend the rest of her life finding ways to make her miserable because I resented her that much. Instead of wasting time on that, I might as well eliminate her ass now.

Chapter 4
Wylde

"You did good," I assured Qadri as she hopped into the whip in the back seat and took a pull from the baseball sized blunt between my fingers.

We were parked a block over from the Byers estate. She and Rollo, one of Rose's connects in the police department, had just rolled out from their assignment. I had known Qadri since she was about twelve, and if she was nearby, she was always down for a mission. When I gave her the situation, she was just finishing a job in Chicago and said she would fly right in. We arrived at about the same time.

"I tried to make sure we got as much of the layout as we could. I know you said your boy pulled the prints for the house too, so you have all the exits as well. The kids are alive, but I could tell something had them shaken. There was no sign of the woman, though. Him and the mother were intense too," she reported. "Rollo counted six guards on the perimeter, and I'm pretty sure Elim is armed too. I could tell how he moved."

Qadri had always been observant; that's how I knew she was the best person for the job. She thought quickly on her feet. Her beauty was another reason she was able to get into certain places. She had a camera on the badge reel she wore, so I was able to peep how Elim was ogling her when he didn't think she was looking. A nigga like him was always looking for the next thing. He said that he and Shayne had a fight, but I wasn't buying that either. Storm and Santana were far too rigid.

"Oh, there's also cameras inside too. I will say it appears to just be him and his mother with the kids. There might be a few staff members in there too."

"Thanks, Qadri." Fisting my beard, I stared ahead, but I could feel shorty watching me.

"You must really care about her."

"My main concern is the kids," I insisted, spiraling my head towards her.

She, more than anyone, knew how I gave it up behind people who couldn't defend themselves. I could be heartless in a lot of ways, but when it came to defenseless people, it set off all my alarms. Qadri simpered and batted her big brown eyes before shaking her head.

"You're a good man, Wylde, contrary to what anyone thinks. I have known that since I was twelve years old. You go hard for the people who mean something to you. I get it, the kids mean something, but you wouldn't care if it wasn't for her," Qadri responded. "I've known you to be with a few women in life... Kaori, Billie, and some others. I know you are capable of love, but to me it never quite seemed like you were *in love*. I have heard that there is a difference."

"What yo' young ass know about it?" I teased, making her crack an innocent smile. "Let me find out you out here giving some nigga hope."

"I ain't say all that." Qadri tittered. "I just ain't never known you to go to these lengths over anybody, other than me."

My cell rang, and Wood's name popped up. Swiping to answer, I brought the phone to my ear.

"What's up, bro?"

"We assembled for the night. We ride at eleven p.m.," my brother reported.

"Bet." I quickly hung up and set the phone in my lap.

I went into my pocket and pulled out a knot of cash that I tossed across the seat. Qadri caught it between both hands.

"I appreciate you, ma. Take care of yourself."

"You know me." She flashed that million-dollar smile and hopped out of the car.

Another vehicle rolled up alongside mine, and she jumped into the passenger seat. There was no telling when I would see her again. Shorty was always in the wind, checking in whenever she took the time to slow down. I didn't sweat it or stress, though, because I knew if nobody else could take care of themselves, Qadri could. If she needed anything, she knew that she could call me, and I would drop it all in a heartbeat if it meant protecting her.

She left me with plenty to think about as I drove back to Rose's safehouse to regroup. I anticipated bloodshed tonight, and it had me anxious, unable to think about anything else. Wood sat on the couch in the safehouse when I stepped inside, and the smell of kush was heavy in the air. I could hear the rest of the crew in the back, and the smell of food cooking also permeated the air. Taking off my coat, I tossed it on the back of a chair and went to grab a glass to fill with whiskey.

"Qadri good?" Wood questioned.

She was something like a baby sister to us both.

"Yeah. On to the next mission." I gulped the Jack Daniels and went to join him.

"What's on your mind?"

"I don't know," I replied, shaking my head. "I don't know

what to think or feel or none of that right now. Shit is just fucked up. What I do know is, those kids don't deserve none of this. I can't imagine what they're going through. Shayne ain't blameless in this either. She put them at risk. I can't just forget that."

Wood passed the blunt to me, and we faced it together while having a drink. Rose and his crew had hooked some food up, so we all sat around shooting the shit and eating before I went to get cleaned up and ready for the night. It was 10:30, and I was in the master bedroom with guns spread over the bed as I locked the bulletproof vest around myself and threw my t-shirt on over it.

Wood tapped at the door before poking his head in.

"You ready?"

"Yeah." I grabbed the Glock off the bed, cocked one back and tucked it.

We rolled up on the block over from the Byer's estate in a fleet of all black Suburbans. The neighborhood was quiet, but a couple of dogs started barking as we unloaded.

"Y'all know the play. We dropping everybody but the kids," Wood reminded them as his ski mask rested cocked to the side on the top of his head. "We're looking for the woman too. Y'all all got the picture of her. If you find her, keep her alive."

There were a bunch of nods as we all pulled the masks down and split up between the two large houses. We were taking the back way to the Byers' estate. They wouldn't know what hit 'em when we were done. I had gone against worse families before, and it appeared Elim's didn't too much care about him since it was just him and his mother around. From what I gathered, his father was a sucka ass nigga too. The nigga had a whole other bitch, and they had a family too, that he kept separate from his wife and their grown children. The stories I heard about Caterina Byers weren't pretty so I imagined he was doing that for many reasons.

On the flight back, I dug deep into my research on the entire family. I knew his brother Evan was a hot head and that he and Elim often got into it in the streets. Neither of them seemed to take the family loyalty to heart. I was always told, even if you didn't get along with your people, you didn't do it out in the open for the world to see. You handled your shit behind closed doors out of respect for the family. These days, mothafuckas didn't get that, though. This generation was actually one of the most disrespectful.

In a matter of minutes, like some high action movie, Rose and his sharp shooters took out the back guards, giving us room to move around and get to the three in the front holding it down. While they did that, Wood managed to pick the lock to the French doors in the kitchen, so we could infiltrate our way inside.

"You go upstairs. I'll check around down here. Meet back here in five minutes. If either of us finds them, we get them out first," I carefully instructed.

The place was massive, and around every corner after we split, I was aiming my gun at some expensive ass statue or staring at some old painting on the walls. Descending the steps of the basement, my heart ramped in my chest and pounded in my ears as I neared the bottom. Not sure which direction to go, I made the choice and drifted to my right nearing a large white door with a lock on it. When I reached down, I couldn't get it open, which frustrated me as I peered around the empty hall. Something was off.

As I took a step back, prepared to just kick the door in, someone came at me from behind. The thin wire around my neck instantly tightened, making me lose grip on my gun as it clattered against the concrete floor.

Fighting for air, I clawed at the calloused hands, but this mothafucka had the strength of a warrior as the wire buried itself into my skin, cutting through my circulation. I couldn't go out like this. Reaching behind me, my hands fell on the facial hair of a man, and immediately, I went for his eyes with my thumbs. His screams and the way his body wiggled behind me let me know I had hit the mark, and his grasp on me finally began to loosen. Choking for air, I sucked in deep breaths with my hands on my knees and spun around to see who had come for me.

"I knew you wouldn't let this go. I thought maybe you got the picture when you came here, and she told you to your face what it was. Clearly, you need some reinforcements. That's my bitch. Has been since I busted that untouched, pretty pussy open. I'm the father of her children, the first nigga she ever loved. She gon' always remember me! Even when she don't want to," Elim growled as he attempted to swing and connect with my face.

His fist landed in the wall beside me instead, and now there was resistance as he tried to pull it from the sheetrock. After sending my forehead crashing into his in a headbutt, I watched him spiral across the hall into the opposite wall before doubling over with groans of pain. Reaching for my pistol at my feet, once it touched my hands, I aimed right for his chest. Blood leaked down his chin as his arms went up, and a slow grin curved the corners of his bleeding mouth.

Pow!

The wounded grunt was followed by choking sounds. I lowered my gun as he slid to the floor, his body tipping over to one side. Stepping closer, I knelt to search his pockets. When I came across a ring of keys, I pulled them out and glanced at the door over my shoulder. Still toting the gun, I tried every single key, and none of them worked until I got to the last one.

The lock turned, and I anxiously spun the knob to open it. At first, I didn't see anything, and the room was bare, with just the dim yellow light above. As I took another step inside, my heart tanked, damn near sinking into my stomach as I spotted Shayne lying on her side on the floor. She was so still, I couldn't tell if she was even breathing as I rushed over to her. Kneeling, I checked for a pulse and couldn't find one, but her body was still warm. I scooped her into my arms and carried her out of the room as gunfire erupted upstairs. Stepping over Elim's lifeless body, I carried Shayne up the staircase and paused in the kitchen.

"Where the fuck you think you going with her?" a low, sultry voice questioned as the barrel of a pistol rested in my side. "Where is my son?"

"Might want to go check on him," I replied, remaining stiff.

I wasn't dumb. I knew if I moved, she could end my life.

"Elim!" Standing at the top of the staircase, she called down, but was met with silence. "All of this because of this bitch! I told him she was trouble. He should never have put one baby in her, let alone two. Bitches like her don't add to you. All they do is take." Elim's mother is who I assumed was behind me. "You probably think she's worth it too." Her comical laugh almost turned hysterical. "Trust me, she's not. Before Elim got with her, he was set to take over from his father and run every-thing. I was going to help him. His brother doesn't want the throne; he just likes to play in the street. His father is nothing but a lying, conniving, manipulative ass nigga living a double life. Shayne was always in his ear, and I believe she set him up right along with her own family because that's the type of scan-dalous ass bitch she is. She used those kids as weapons against us because she knows how we feel about family. That bitch doesn't get to walk away from this! Not this time!"

I didn't have access to my gun, so when I turned abruptly, I used my leg strength to send that bitch flying backward down the staircase to her basement. She didn't tuck and roll, so I knew her injuries would be severe. A shot fired from her gun, barely missing a nigga's head as it shattered the light fixture above her island counter in the kitchen. The woman landed in a pile, and her gun slid across the concrete floor. I didn't bother to stick around and check for a pulse as footsteps stampeded in my direction from the front of the house. The way she was mangled would either kill a mothafucka or they would wish they were dead. Seeing Wood with Storm in his arms and Santana not far behind took a heavy weight off my chest.

"Let's go." My brother caught one look at Shayne in my arms and kept it pushing to the same doors we entered through not long ago.

Storm's worry ridden expression as she took in her mother in my arms broke my heart. With her whimpering and San clinging to Wood's shirt, I trailed them outside. The wind picked up, rustling the trees right before the clouds shifted, thunder roared, and rain slowly began to fall over us. Once we got everyone back to the cars, I asked Rose to meet us at the safehouse with someone who had medical expertise. Shayne hadn't woken up, which had me worried because I did confirm she was breathing as her chest rose and fell. It was like she was in a comatose state or heavily sedated, and I wanted to be sure she was going to be okay. We had gone through all this and although a part of me was livid with how she had gone about things, the bigger part of me didn't care and just wanted her to be okay.

Shayne

My eyelids had to weigh a ton as I attempted to flicker them open. I couldn't shake that lethargic, fatigued feeling either. I was barely able to move my tongue because my mouth was so dry. Curling up on my side, I couldn't be sure where I was, and I didn't want to open my eyes to find out. The chilly atmosphere had my teeth chattering as I clutched my aching stomach.

The fuck is going on?

I couldn't lift my head. Every muscle in my body ached, sending painful groans through my throat. I was dying. I had to be. The stabbing pains in my belly were going to take me out.

"Shayne! Shayne!" Nael's voice was a comfort, but he was stern as his big hands grabbed my shoulders, forcing me to sit up.

When he pulled me into his chest, the aroma of his familiar scent drifted up my nose and caused my eyes to flicker open. I held onto his flannel shirt, burying my face in his chest as I erupted into weeping. The last three years of my life played out like a box office film, rocking me back into reality.

"What's wrong?" He swept his hand over my hair, smoothing it out in an effort to comfort me.

"He's going to kill me. He's going to kill everyone." I clung to Nael as a sob broke through my vocal cords.

"Shhh. Nobody is going to hurt you. You know where you are?"

His question gave me pause as my eyes finally managed to open and adjust to the warm lighting.

The room was so vast, and I was resting in a large bed with big oak bed posts. A set of doors was to my right, leading to a balcony from what I could see. I was on the second story, and my eyes curiously darted around.

"What happened? How did I get here?" With a racing heart, I pressed a hand against my chest and took in a deep breath.

Everything was so jumbled in my head. This very moment seemed like a mere mirage of my imagination.

"You don't remember anything?" Nael's striking teddy bear brown eyes scrutinized me. He stood and went to grab a bottle of water for me from the table on the other side of the bed.

Easing back into the pile of pillows behind me, I rigidly popped right back up as a tall, stern looking older gentleman marched inside. He had slim features, like the rapper Snoop. His angular face and long nose with the pointed tip were very defined. I got doctor vibes from him as he stood at my side, examining me, and brought the cold metal part of the stethoscope against my chest.

"Is everything okay?" he asked, narrowing both eyes.

"She just woke up screaming. I think it was just a bad dream," Nael spoke up.

"Are you okay, Shayne? Are you in any pain? Do you need something?"

Nael held the bottle of water for me to take, which I did. Twisting the cap off, I took big gulps and caught my breath after swallowing.

"Where are my kids? I need to see them," I finally managed to speak.

"They're downstairs with Wood," Nael chimed in. "I'll go get them."

"I am Dr. Wilson. You can call me Screw." The dark skinned Ethiopian looking man greeted me with a warm smile while applying one of those blood pressure readers to my arm. "You have been through a lot."

"Hmm, how can you tell?"

"There were very large amounts of narcotics in your system. A lot of them didn't mix well." He nodded to the cup I was gulping like my last drink. "I provided a detox water. A little ginger, some aloe vera, and cucumber. Little things like that can flush those drugs out."

"Well, Screw... what else can you tell me? You seem to have all the answers." He checked my numbers as they popped on his reader and gave a nod before removing it from my arm.

"I'm a doctor first. My main concern is always the patient. Depending on how long you have been using, withdrawals are going to take you on a downward spiral. You need to be prepared for it. I was also able to run your blood and urine through a private lab. It was all necessary for a tox screen to figure out what was in your blood stream. Everything came back conclusive. It seems you are also seven weeks pregnant. I didn't bring it to anyone's attention. I thought it was your news to deliver, and I wasn't sure you were aware."

"I appreciate your discretion." I sipped the water and swallowed. "I have been through a lot, as you mentioned. If you saw the tox screen then you know—"

"What I know is, you and this baby could be a lot worse off," Screw assured. "I've been a doctor for a long time, Shayne. I have seen many cases, some good and bad. You are one of the lucky ones. When you get home, follow up with your primary care physician." He smiled as the door to the room creaked open.

The beat of my heart stalled when I laid eyes on Wylde. So much had happened. It had been over a month, yet everything had changed. Screw lifted himself from the bed.

"She seems to be doing well. Let's keep her hydrated. We can try some food for breakfast. I'll be back to check on her in about an hour."

"Thanks, Screw," Wylde responded, eyes fixed on me as the doctor cleared the room.

"You seem to have a habit of saving me." I was doing my

best to keep the mood light, but it was obvious from his lack of expression that he was there for something else.

He had a rebuttal, but the sweetest sound in the world filled my ears as Storm and Santana raced past him into the room with Nael not far behind. They both leapt onto the bed to rush me with hugs.

"Mommy!" Storm threw her arms around me, and San rested his head against my chest while holding me. "You're okay!"

My heart was full as I held them and kissed the top of both their heads. It seemed like it had been so long since we had this type of interaction. I hated being kept from them, even living in the same house. Caterina had locks on their doors and a key just like Elim had for me. We were all allowed out at certain times of the day for interaction. The fact that Elim was okay with that was most disturbing.

"So much better now that I can see you and hold you." I wrapped her in the tightest hug.

"Grandma Cat said Daddy was going to hurt you and we would never see you again!" Storm pulled away to look at me.

"Hey, I'm fine. Look at me. I know I don't look the best, but I'm here. I know everything has been scary over the last few weeks, but I promise to never put you in that position again," I vowed.

"Can we go home now?" Storm asked, but looked at Wylde when she did so. "I want to sleep in my own bed and play with all my toys."

"Soon as the doctor clears your mama for travel, we can go," Wylde assured them.

"Come on, let's go make sure we got everything packed and get your mama some breakfast. I'll be downstairs if you need me." Nael led the kids away, leaving Wylde and I in the room with piles of tension as thick as mud between us.

"How are you feeling?" he asked, dressed in all black as he approached the side of the bed.

"I'm okay. I think I'm strong enough to get home." The distance between us was obvious in that moment. "You could have left us in that house and not looked back. I don't know how you showed up when you did, but... for that, I am grateful. There were days I wasn't sure I was going to make it to the next."

"And you couldn't trust me enough to tell me the truth after everything I've done for you?" He spoke evenly as a contemptuous stare stretched across his face.

Wylde had been a few things with me: attentive, caring, passionate. He had never been genuinely angry though, until now. Tears flickered behind my gaze.

"Storm called Wood's phone. It's the only reason we knew to come. You put not only yourself at risk, but both of them!" His outrage caused me to flinch.

"I didn't have a lot of choice in the matter," I snapped, growing agitated by how he was basically condemning me for some shit that was out of my control. "And I don't like this conversation."

"Why is that? Too much truth for you?" he asked, tilting his head.

"Truth?" I scoffed, biting down a harsh laugh. "You can get out. It's easy for you to lay all this at my feet and make it all my fault when this mothafucka snatched me and my kids and threatened everything else I gave a damn about! Including you. Instead of giving me the benefit of the doubt, you chose to believe all the lies this nigga spread about me over the years, just like everyone else. So, fuck you and your *truth*, Wylde."

"The fuck was I supposed to think when you just left, and the next time I see you it's with him!" The insolence behind his eyes rocked me to my core.

It wasn't long ago that he peered at me with nothing but admiration.

"You were supposed to know, Wylde! What can I expect, though? You the same man I caught hugged up with another bitch." I caught the flicker of anger bounce across his orbs as he locked his jaw. "That's what I thought. You standing there lecturing me about trust, and you can't deliver on that your damn self. Do you even know what you want? Is it me, is it Billie, or maybe it's Kaori. Sounds like you have some things to figure out. I spent the last month in a living hell, being drugged everyday so that I remained compliant, being kept from my children and locked away like some prisoner, having to..." The thought of Elim inside me triggered rage as my blood boiled. "You know what... just get the fuck out. I can't do this right now."

His thick brows knitted together as he caught my attitude buried underneath my nonchalance. Not only that, but I was hurt beyond what I wanted him to see. With piercing eyes canvassing me, I noticed his hostility seemed to fade as empathy replaced it. My little rant seemed to have gotten to him as he bowed his head humbly.

Avoiding his stare, I rested against the pillows and turned on my side. I gave him my back as my heart cracked open in my chest. This type of heartbreak was new for me. I had brought enough drama to his life in such a short time. Right now, it seemed like all we could do was go our separate ways, whatever the hell that looked like. The only other person responsible for where we were other than Elim, was myself. Wylde was entitled to what he harbored inside. The situation was fucked up in every way. I might have escaped Elim and his torture, but I would never be the same, and I wasn't sure what to do or where to go next.

The flight back to Greenwich was tense, to say the least. Nael sat with the kids on one side of the plane, and they were chattering away like nothing had happened. Seated near a window, I stared out at the sky as we cruised through the air. It was kind of comforting as I sat with one leg propped up in the seat as I wrapped an arm around my knee and got lost in my own mind. The weariness hadn't worn off, and every now and then, I would catch a chill and hug myself in the hoodie that I wore. No lie, my body had adjusted to being high all the time, and I craved something to push me through this stressful time. I couldn't even have a drink since hearing the doctor's news.

My mind was all over the place, and I was under a microscope as far as I was concerned with the way everyone kept checking on me. Sipping from a bottle of water, I pulled my hoodie over my head, brought my legs under me, and crossed my arms over my chest in an effort to stay warm. When a solid figure slid into the seat beside me and set down a tray of food between our seats, I glanced up and was met with Wood's grim-faced stare. I couldn't read his expression as he eased the cold cut sandwich, chips, and a plate of veggies and dip over to me.

"I'm not hungry," I muttered and turned away from him.

I hadn't forgotten our last conversation, and since I was mad at Wylde, it was going to pour over onto him too.

"I'm trying to make peace, 'cause I was thinking the worst about you—"

"I don't need your pity or sympathy, Wood. Keep that same energy," I voiced, impaling him with a blistering glare before directing my eyes back out my window.

"I was wrong to insinuate anything about Wylde and Kaori." Wood sighed.

"No, you were right. It damn sure opened my eyes. Seems like there's a lot of that going around."

"On some real shit, I was wrong. I was fucked up and in my head about the shit with Lishan, and I took it out on you. For that, I'm sorry. You ain't deserve that. I wish you felt you could count on us, though. After everything we've done for you and those kids, we fam—"

"That's exactly why I didn't say anything. I watched what he did to my parents, my brother. I knew he wouldn't hesitate to do the same to you or Wylde. I thought I was protecting you." My neck swiveled, sending my head pivoting in his direction.

When our eyes locked this time, Wood's filled with understanding before he nodded.

"You a real one, sis. No doubt. Get your rest."

Curling up in the seat, I took a couple of bites from the sandwich and had some juice before dozing off. Images of Elim danced in my head, causing me to toss and turn and eventually snap awake in a cold sweat while my heart threatened to beat out of my chest.

"No!" I screamed, startling everyone on the plane as I shot up in my seat.

When I realized where I was, I rested a hand against my chest, and my eyes darted around skeptically. My children were still on the other side, both gaping at me with wide eyes. Sitting up, I caught my breath before dropping my face into my hands. I was unraveling silently while rocking back and forth. Elim had left me traumatized.

"You might need this." Wylde set a glass of tequila on the small tray between the two seats.

"No, I'm fine. Thanks." The aroma of the alcohol struck my nostrils, causing my stomach to flip as I leaned back.

"Shayne, you shaking, mama."

"Don't do that." I shook my head.

I couldn't deal with him right now, especially being all attentive. The familiar warmth in his eyes was there, hidden behind his evident concern.

"Do what? Care? You can't just turn that shit off. Trust me, I tried." He lowered himself into the seat beside me since Wood was now hanging with Nael and the kids.

With misting eyes, I peered into his. For a moment, we had gone back in time. I didn't want to tell him about the baby. It would open a new set of issues between us, and I didn't want him putting in an effort just because I was carrying his child. Unsure of how to process this myself, I was going to need some time. *How do I tell him?* There were so many things swirling in my mind that it was hard to keep up. The closer we got to home, the more anxious and nauseated I became.

"I care. But... it's not always enough, is it?" I asked, glancing his way.

"Only time will tell." Wylde slouched and tossed the shot back.

Not many words passed between us on the rest of the flight. I recalled getting sleepy again and dozing off. The next thing I knew, I was being nudged awake and lifting my head off Wylde's shoulder. Suddenly well rested and starving, I straightened up in my seat and stretched while his intoxicating copper brown eyes drank me in.

"Time to go home," he told me.

I came alive on the drive from the landing strip to the house. Nael, the kids, and Wood all went ahead of me as we unloaded from the car. Wylde wasn't far behind as I stopped and soaked in the house. It was just like I remembered it, bringing a smile to my lips. This was home. We were planting roots here. This house held some good memories so far, and I wanted to keep those and add more. Wylde was so close to me that his body heat radiated off mine as he dropped a hand against my hip and brought his chin over my shoulder. Growing taut under his touch, my eyes involuntarily shut. He was peace, even now.

"This is where you belong."

Facing him, I stood on my toes and drew him closer. My lips meshed into his as he pulled me to him, leaving no space between us as our tongues deepened the kiss. I was mad, pissed off, all of that, but at the same time, I was grateful.

"I missed you," Wylde said against my lips before pressing his forehead against mine.

"I missed you too," I voiced, sucking on his bottom lip affectionately as he cupped my chin and fed me his tongue. "I fucked up, mama. I'll spend every day making it right."

"Can you just stay here tonight with us for starters? I think it would make me and the kids feel better."

"Whatever you want." His juicy lips apprehended mine again, and we turned, fighting off the chill in the air to get inside.

I knew things weren't going to be perfect, but in this moment, it didn't matter. I was being selfish. It wasn't just me wanting him close. He made me feel secure. It was a necessity for my mental health. I was bound to be up all night, checking the doors and windows until I drove myself crazy. For some reason, even though I had been told Elim was dead, I didn't get any finality in that. He still had an entire family that was going to hold someone responsible for what happened to him and his mother.

Chapter 5
Lishan

It was almost four in the afternoon, and I was packing things around the small apartment so I could get the hell out of here. I wanted nothing more than to sleep, but I had to grab our medical records and a couple of other mementos that meant something to us. Sighing, I grabbed my cell phone off the coffee table just as the door to the apartment opened. The guard that had been posted stepped aside so Myra could enter.

"Well, looks like you are ready to jet out of here." She perked up. "Where you heading?"

"What do you want?"

"Listen, Lishan, we are done with the games and back and forth, sweetie. Now, we people because of your mama, but that don't mean I don't expect certain things from people who work for me."

"I can resolve that for you. I don't work for you anymore." I tied my bag shut and looked her in the face.

"What are you going to do?" Myra studied me. "You don't

have shit, Lishan! You ain't shit without me or Merlin. Don't make me force my hand on this. We had a deal."

"We didn't sign a fucking contract, Myra! I can leave any time I fucking feel like. You and Merlin don't own me! I said I'm done."

"You might want to reconsider. Don't forget we still got your initiation video. I bet this mothafucka will run up the views and get us paid. We could tag you and everything." A scandalous grin turned up the corners of her mouth.

Her audacity was astounding. I was seventeen when I first started working for Myra and doing parties. Every girl back then had to be recorded for her audition, which Merlin took the pleasure of doing. I had forgotten all about it until just now. The idea that it would be leaked for the world to see was gut-wrenching.

"Is that what we're doing? You blackmailing me?"

"Call it what you want, sweetie. This is where we are. This reminds me of your mother." She tittered and shook her head. "She had a situation with your father back in the day. Yeah, ya mama went looking for him to tell him about you and try to get some money out of him. Instead, she found his wife and children. Imagine that. The wife paid her and told her to leave and don't ever come back. So, that's exactly what she did."

The mention of my sperm donor caught my attention. I didn't know much about him. The only thing my mama ever told me was that he was passing through, they fucked around, and she ended up pregnant. I assumed he was just another deadbeat, not that he never knew about me.

"Don't be like her, or me, for that matter. Get your money and leave these niggas where the fuck they are."

"You know what? I've spent the last three years taking orders from you, taking the small cuts when you want to skim off the top for your percentage. Demeaning myself for fucking scraps, and I'm still living in the projects, trying to get by. Do what you want to do with that video, Myra, just remember one thing. I was a minor. That means you could be charged for having that footage. Think about that while you try to get your roster up."

When Wood pushed the door open, I was so happy to see him. I could tell he was exhausted, but his warm eyes immediately turned hard when he caught Myra lingering nearby.

"Hey," I greeted him. "I didn't know you were back. How did you know I was here?"

"Come on, shorty. That's my man on you. The fuck she doing here?" His face balled up bitterly while strolling inside.

"She was just leaving. Right, Myra?" I checked with her, feigning a smile as she forced one across her lips.

"Remember you made this choice, Lishan. I can't control Merlin or how he chooses to react to this."

"Ain't nobody worried about yo' bitch ass son. Tell that nigga he got a problem, man the fuck up and come to me. Lishan and her family are under my protection, and I don't negotiate when it comes to looking out for mine. The name is Woodrow Katri. Ask about me." Wood's hand rested on his hip as a glower broke across his face while his eyes narrowed into slits.

Myra cocked a brow. Wood was an alpha male, nothing like her bitch ass son, and it was obvious in his words and actions as far as I was concerned. Clearly, she picked up on it too as she adjusted the strap to her purse on her shoulder and stepped closer to the door.

"You didn't have to do that," I muttered as Wood came up and grabbed my bag off the couch.

"Fuck that. They need to know you got somebody riding for you. Ain't shit for you to fear walking around here because if anybody fucks with you, they answer to me." He kissed the top of my head and tossed the strap to my bag over his shoulder. "Let's go."

Once we were settled in his car, cruising the cold, winter streets, it was obvious he was taking us back to what we now considered home. Just like that, my siblings and I had been uprooted. The looks on their faces when they saw the layout of the spacious four bedroom, full basement home was picture worthy. It made me happy to see them happy, and Wood wasn't about to let any of us go anywhere if he wasn't involved. Overnight, he had become my provider and protector.

"I talked to Wylde. He said he was good with y'all staying and making the place home."

"Wood, I can't afford that," I argued.

"Who the fuck said I was accepting a payment, Lis?" His head swung toward me. "He's going to stay at the house with Shayne and the kids, anyway."

Lighting up, I had to catch my breath as I swung toward him in the seat.

"Shayne's back? Is she okay? Are the kids okay? Why didn't you say anything until now?" I swatted him, and he flinched while rubbing the spot where I hit him.

"She's fine, physically. They all are. I was gon' tell you when we got to the house. It's been a long twenty-four hours, shorty. I need something good to eat and a shower. I'm glad you got all your shit out of that spot, though. Leave the past right there." He extended his arm across the seat and rested a big hand on my thigh as he gave it a squeeze.

"What happened when you went to get her?" I questioned.

"Her fuck ass baby daddy and his mama had her and the kids locked up like some hostages. Shayne was in the basement; she was also being drugged. The kids were upstairs with locks on their doors to keep them inside. Shit was ill." He shook his head and swiped his beard.

"Oh, my God. Poor Shayne, and those kids. I can't imagine," I muttered. "I want to see her."

"Tomorrow or give it a few days. Both of you have been through enough. She's out of it and has a lot to process. Her and Wylde gotta work through their shit. I honestly don't know what's gon' happen there. Ain't like he been sitting around, pining and crying over her. Yeah, the shit hurt, but he damn sure ain't been lonely. I don't know how Shayne's gon' feel about that after everything she's been through."

"Damn, that is a lot."

"Shit got real, but Shayne is strong. Her kids are resilient as hell. It will take some time, but they'll be fine."

We arrived at the house a few minutes later. Wood parked inside his garage and grabbed our bags from the car. The aroma of food wafted over us, and my stomach immediately growled as we entered the kitchen together. Ledger stood at the stove, whipping it up with several pots going and a dish towel draped over his shoulder while he worked.

"Oh, shit, its Ledge Boyardee." Wood dropped our bags at the door and went over to the stove to see what was cooking. "Damn, this shit smells good. I'm about to go get cleaned up. A nigga gon' need a plate of whatever that is."

"It's parmesan crusted chicken with pasta and marinara sauce. I made garlic bread too."

"My nigga." Wood rubbed his hands together and grinned eagerly. "Lis, find something for us to watch 'cause it's a wrap after this."

"Where are Linc and Lumi?" I asked, accepting Wood's kiss and slap to my ass while he bypassed me and went into the hallway.

"In their room, doing homework. Misael is sleeping, so I decided to take care of dinner. I knew you would probably be tired after going to the apartment. I got some money saved up from working."

"You are one of the most considerate people I know, bro. Don't ever change that." I admired him from across the counter.

"Just looking out for y'all l ike I'm supposed to. Hey, I want to go shopping and get me some new gear. Is it cool if I go tomorrow with a few friends?" he requested.

For the last month, things had been normal for us. Living in the hotel was great with all their amenities and everything. Since I was still recovering, it was perfect, and the kids loved it. Over time, it started to get a little crowded, and I knew that Linc and Lumi wanted to go outside and play like normal kids. Him and Wylde told me to move into the house. His brother wasn't quite ready to move on after everything with Shayne and be alone. I think being around my brothers and sister helped him too in some ways.

Wylde was solid. Despite spiraling and shutting down while Shayne was away, he remained present if I needed him when Wood wasn't available. You just didn't come across those type of men. It was nothing for either of them to provide whatever any of us needed. The kids all had new clothes and shoes, and I loved the fact that they were truly appreciative of it all. I made it clear that none of it was expected, but they insisted. I wasn't one to fight when I wasn't in a position to do it for them myself. Wood wouldn't let me spend a dime if I had it. I told him he didn't have to do all that, but he insisted. Every night, he was here checking on us, making sure me and the baby were good. He didn't exactly say all that, but it was his intention and how he handled me when he was around.

Sometimes I forgot I was pregnant, and it was Wood making sure I was taking my prenatal vitamins and keeping appointments with the doctor. So far, everything seemed fine. We never talked about abortion or anything. It was kind of a given once I left the hospital that I was keeping the baby. He seemed more receptive to all of this than me. My siblings didn't just look to me if they wanted or needed something. If Lumi mentioned something in conversation, Wood would run out and buy it for her. Between her and Storm, he was a certified sucka.

"What friends are those?" I asked, pulling out a chair at the table and sitting down.

"Just Yoni and Chris." Ledger shrugged.

"That should be fine. I can get Lumi and Linc from the bus stop."

"So, are we staying here permanently?" Ledger glanced over his shoulder while stirring something in a pot.

They had been enrolled in their new schools for about two weeks. Wood didn't think they should be missing out on anything, and it gave us all a break from them during the day to do other shit. For me, I was recovering and trying to navigate being pregnant.

"I don't know. I haven't talked to Wood about it. He's being nice for now, but I don't want to burden him with this."

"Is he your man or something?" Ledger queried.

"He's the father of this baby. So, he cares, but that doesn't always mean something."

I played with one of the place mats and thought about the situation while also considering my mother and all the shit she went through to have us. *How am I supposed to do this?* I couldn't depend on Wood. I knew that shit could cost me in the end. If I invested too much and ended up hurt, it wouldn't just be about me.

"He didn't have to do any of this for us, Lis. I think he cares more than you think. You not used to it, and that's why it doesn't feel right."

"What you know about it?" I chucked my chin because he was making a little bit of sense.

"I don't know. I ain't never liked Merlin, and you never had any dudes around us. Wood is dope, and the twins love him. He's like a big kid sometimes."

Tittering, I shook my head at his accuracy. Not sure how it happened, but this man had swooped into my life and charmed everyone. Regardless, I was still waiting for the other shoe to drop. Good things didn't happen to me or my family, so it was a bit nerve wrecking.

"I just think he's good people," Ledger communicated. "We don't have a lot of those in our lives."

"You can say that again."

For the next few minutes, we chopped it up, and Ledger started making plates for everyone.

It didn't take long for Misael to wheel himself into the kitchen. Lumi and Linc weren't far behind him. Ledger had set the table for us and everything in the dining room as Wood strolled inside with his cell against his ear. The chicken had a golden breaded layer of crust and was placed over perfect penne pasta with marina sauce covering it. There was a layer of mozzarella and parmesan blended and melting on top. A side salad had been prepared in each bowl, and I couldn't help but admire Ledger as he moved about the table, setting everyone's plate just right. He really was talented at this cooking shit. I could tell he loved working in that kitchen because he was always whipping something up. We didn't starve around there as long as there was food and Ledger was around.

"Yeah, I'll be there. I got you. Give me a couple of hours," I heard Wood say before hanging up.

"You leaving?" I questioned before saying a quick prayer over my plate as he pulled out the chair beside me where his was already prepared as well.

"Yeah, just some shit I need to handle. I'll be back in the morning."

I wanted to pry, but I didn't want to come off all needy and nosy either, like I was his woman. He had extended a huge courtesy to me and my family, but neither of us had discussed anything further than that. So, we all sat around eating, and I got in my feelings, thinking maybe he was tired of playing house with us and wanting to get his dick wet with the next bitch. Clearly, there was nothing happening with us. Silence filled the table as everyone smashed their meal. Linc and Lumi did most of the talking, about school. Wood was spending every other second on his phone, which caused me to lose my appetite as I thought about how he was going to end his night.

When I stood, I started toward the bedroom that I occupied, which just happened to be Wood's room where he kept all his shit. Misael took the room next to the living room on the first floor, while the kids and I took the top floor. There was a bonus room, which was just enough room for a twin bunk bed for Lumi, a dresser with a built-in desk below, and a TV mounted to the wall. There was an adjoining bathroom with the boys across the way, and I was on the other side of the hall. It was nice having the space, and Lumi absolutely loved having her own room, even if it was compact. Sometimes Linc would still come and sleep on the floor with her, though.

Grabbing a few items from the dresser where I stored my clothes, I pulled out a long-sleeved, oversized t-shirt from PINK and fuzzy socks as the door was pushed open and Wood let himself inside.

"Man, that little nigga needs his own food truck or some shit. Homie got skills." He rubbed his full belly as I strolled toward the bathroom door, unresponsive.

It still smelled like his soap in the room, and I hated that. I hated that I was still attracted to him. The longer I walked around pregnant with his child, the easier it would be to fall even harder. It was frustrating as hell lying next to him at night, but he was handling me like I was some duty he had to perform instead of a man who was interested in what we could be.

"The fuck wrong with you?"

"Nothing," I answered before letting myself into the bathroom.

When I tried to slam the door in his face, he placed his foot between the door and the frame to stop me.

"Nothing got you around here pouting and about to slam the door in my face?"

"Why the fuck do you care, Wood? Weren't you leaving for the night?"

He swiped his beard and tried to calm himself as I stood there with my arms tucked across my tender and swollen breasts, waiting for his rebuttal.

"Is that what this is about? You mad I'm leaving?"

"You just got back. Where you going that's so important, and why you staying out all night?" I questioned, sounding way too damn invested.

His handsome face fell into a simper that I wanted to slap the fuck off.

"This shit is funny to you?" I sneered, my perfectly plucked brows drawing together.

"Nah, but you are." He chuckled. "Them hormones got you buggin'."

"Fuck you!"

I was ready to shut the door on him once again, but this time, his large hand pressed against the oak, causing it not to budge.

"Calm the fuck down! And that's the last time you gon' try to slam a fucking door in my face. The fuck wrong with you?"

"Why don't you go fuck on your little bitch and leave me alone? I never should have moved in here. I knew—"

"You knew what?" Biting into his bottom lip and locking his jaw, he inched into my space. "You don't even know what the fuck you talking about right now, and you never asked where I was going."

"Because it's not my business."

"Then why do you care, Lis? Closed mouths don't get fed, baby. Speak your mind around here, 'cause I damn sure ain't no fucking Dionne Warwick or Miss Cleo around this mothafucka."

I hated the emotions that were coursing through me. I had gone from enraged to hurt in a matter of minutes. Now, I wanted to burst into tears because he was being aggressive.

"I don't want to talk to you," I muttered.

"Don't get quiet now. You had all that fucking attitude before. If you want to know something, all you gotta do is ask. I don't lie to you."

When our eyes met this time, I was still indifferent, and his arrogant stance had me ready to mush his head back. His dark eyes challenged me, daring me to speak up as my shoulders dropped, and my gaze fell to the ground. His sturdy presence and defined muscles were so sexy as I absorbed him. Hooking his finger through the belt loop of my jeans, he tugged me to him while studying my disgruntled expression.

"I'm going to the club. The construction crew is working late tonight, and Dalvin wants me there to oversee things. That's it. I ain't going to see no bitch or none of that." Sloping forward, his juicy lips fell over mine in a soul snatching kiss that sent electric sparks from the tip of my toes to my pulsing clit. It had been a while since we had been together, and I missed it. Deepening the kiss with his tongue, Wood fisted some of my hair and finally released me.

"Okay," I whispered, playing with the chain against his chest before he tilted my chin so I was looking into his magnetic orbs.

"You good?"

"I guess." I gave an eyeroll.

"Don't guess, Lis. Let me know how you feel, shorty. Don't bottle that shit up. Keep it a buck. You know a nigga like me ain't sensitive."

"I just..." Letting go of a heavy sigh, I shook my head. "Nevermind."

"What I say?" he challenged.

"What are we doing, Wood? You moved us in here, and you're taking care of us. I don't know what to think. This shit is starting to feel normal, and—"

"What's wrong with that, Lis? Because you not used to it?"

"Now you sound like Ledger." I simpered.

"He's pretty wise to be as young as he is. Little nigga got more heart than men twice his age. That's why I kept him off the street. I know he means something to you, and I see his potential. I ain't the type that's gon' go around singing shit off the rooftops, but I thought what was between us didn't need to be explained. You carrying my seed. Of course, I care about you and what matters to you. I fucked up when I first found out what you were out there doing. I didn't give you a chance to explain, and I didn't want to see that maybe there was a method to your madness. Most bitches I know are just scandalous by nature, and I grew to expect that. That ain't you, Lis. Not by a long shot."

His little speech had me tearing up as he planted the softest peck to my waiting lips.

"I never thought all those late nights up with you would lead to this. I've never let anyone into my life because it was a trigger for me. You fit so naturally. It's kind of scary."

"Don't ever be afraid to let me in or let me take care of you. I get that it's something you're used to, but now you can adjust to letting a mothafucka do right by you."

"Myra said something to me, and I don't know how to take it." The faintest glimmer of a frown creased my forehead.

"I don't like that bitch or her son. Shit is hot right now because of the shit with Shayne, so I'm taking my time, but I'll deal with them."

"It's not just that. She mentioned my daddy, who I never knew. She basically said he had a wife and a whole family out there. The wife knew about me, paid my mother off, and they never told him. He doesn't even know I exist," I expressed, a little agitated by the idea and curious. It was frustrating as hell not to have anyone to talk to about it.

"Damn, that's cold. You think she's telling the truth?"

"I don't know, and I... maybe Misael knows something." A light bulb went off as I peered into Wood's eyes.

"Maybe. Talk to him. If you need me to use my resources, you know I got you. I don't want your hopes to get high on this, though. Take it with a grain of salt and do your own research."

"What if I have family out there? They never knew about me. This man doesn't know about me. I could have siblings, or more siblings, I should say. I don't know, it's kind of wild to think about." I shook away my thoughts as Wood locked his lean arms around me and kissed my neck.

"Don't stress yourself out over it. If it's meant to be, it will be. Between the plane ride and that meal, I need to reset."

"Okay. I'm going to take a shower too. I'll be in there."

By the time I got out of the shower fifteen minutes later ,his ass was already curled up and sleeping. Shaking my head, I got dressed and decided to grab something to drink before turning in myself. Lately, I had been making this smoothie recipe that I found on TikTok, and it was so fire that I had to have one damn near every day. Padding down the stairs, I found everyone in the living room around the TV, tuning in to Abbott Elementary. Misael was in his wheelchair next to the couch, where the twins were laid out together under a blanket, and Ledger was on the other side, posted on the loveseat with his legs stretched out. They were making themselves right at home, which made me smile. I was at ease here from the moment Wood brought me over for our first session.

"Pop, can I talk to you in the kitchen?"

Misael was slow, but he trailed me down the darkened hall, stopping next to the gray and black square kitchen table seated for four. Standing beside one of the chairs, I fidgeted from foot to foot, and Misael studied me with peculiar eyes.

"What's on your mind?"

"Myra."

"Why you want to talk about that old hoe for?" Misael gave me the screw face, and with those oxygen tubes up his nose, and the way his mouth curled up since he wasn't wearing his dentures, I couldn't help but laugh.

"She said something to me today, and I wanted to ask you about it."

"Okay, what she say?"

"She mentioned my father. Said he never knew about me. Claims that Mama took a payoff from his wife, and she never sought him out again. What you make of that?" I queried, tucking my arms across my chest and tilting my head.

First of all, he averted my eyes, which was a red flag that he knew some shit. Then he did this gruff muttering under his breath as he shook his head.

"I wish ya mama was here to tell you all about it. I thought I would be dead before it ever came up," he grumbled.

"So, it's true?"

"I know she came back with a lot of money. Her and Myra

was living it up like some hot girls in the city. I knew something was up. She cared more about money than being a mother. I wish he had known. Maybe he could have done something," Misael muttered.

"Do you know who he is?"

"Lishan..."

"Misael, this is my father. He doesn't know about me. You don't think that's wrong? If he's out there, I want to know him, and he might want to know me."

"You don't know that. We talking about a married man here anyway," he argued.

"I can't believe that you, as a man, as a father, would even condone this." Shaking my head, he had officially rattled me.

"You don't know this man. Why does it matter now? You're grown. You have lived twenty years without him. What can he do for you now?"

"That isn't your choice to make, just like it wasn't hers. He had a right to know, and so do I!" I aimed a finger at my chest, and my grandpa dropped his head in shame.

I loved him, but he could be stubborn, and if he wasn't confined to that wheelchair, he would be a force. I remembered him before he was ailing and needed help doing everything, and he was very strict. I wouldn't have been able to get away with half the shit I was doing now if he wasn't sick. I didn't want to stress myself out with this argument, so I grabbed a bottle of water from the fridge and went back to the bedroom. Once I climbed into bed with Wood, he pulled me closer on instinct, not even opening his eyes, and I rested my head against his sturdy chest. My mind was running a race from one thing to the next but listening to his strong heartbeat ended up coaxing me to sleep.

Wood

Later that night...

After some thought, I decided to join Dalvin in his club venture. The money was good, and I could let him run shit while I just played the back and collected my coins. It was a good way to flush with the other shit Wylde and I made with our gun running paper too. My brother and I lived modestly. I might floss with some jewelry or some gear, but never would a nigga go out and purchase what he was really capable of without raising some red flags.

When I was younger, it was all about the fame. Everybody loves attention. Now, as a grown ass man, I was in fact seeing the bigger picture. Every day, I woke up trying to put shit together to make sure everybody I knew was straight and eating, whether I was there or not. Adding Lishan, her siblings, and eventually a funeral for Misael, I knew that I had to hustle a little harder to secure things.

Whipping the Porsche Cayenne into a parking spot behind the club, I finished smoking my blunt and grabbed the cup of coffee I needed to keep me going tonight. I didn't want to get out of bed. Lishan was feeling good as fuck, and I missed being up in that. Knowing she was also carrying my seed only made me want her more. She had no idea. I knew she was in a fragile state because of her condition, no matter what she said. So, I was doing my best to take my time with her and handle her with care.

"What's good, Wood?" Dalvin tossed his chin and took a pull from his blunt as I got out of the car, fixing my jeans on my waist.

My pistol made these mothafuckas heavy. He was posted on the hood of his car, and I could see the different trucks parked, letting me know the construction crew was already here.

"What up, D? Everything good around here? I didn't expect you."

"Yeah, just wrapping some shit up. Thanks for coming through and keeping an eye on things. Can't trust some of these mothafuckas. So, what you been up to? Nobody ever sees you at the functions. You Mormon now or something?" He cackled, pulling from the blunt again.

"Nah. Just got other shit going on."

"You married? Got kids?"

"Nah, a nigga ain't locked down like that, yet. I got a baby on the way, though."

"Congratulations." Dalvin bobbed his head as the passenger door to his whip slammed shut.

I didn't even know he wasn't alone as I watched the slim figure emerge through the shadows. Taken aback, for a minute, I was rendered speechless as Noemi Blanks' face took me back in time. Baby was still fine, with wide hips, and from where she stood, the ass to match. With her long box braids draping to her derriere, she stuck her hands into the back pockets of her jeans, and the faintest hint of a smirk marred her face.

"What's up, Woodrow?" she greeted me in that raspy voice as her hazel eyes sparkled. Her peanut butter tinted skin was shiny, contrasting with the tattoos that covered one arm and part of her other hand. With a dark makeup look, she was pristine while skimming me hungrily.

"Been a long time, Noemi."

Dalvin stepped up and looped an arm around her waist, drawing her closer to him. Nigga saw the smoldering shadows building in her eyes as she drank me in. She was obvious as fuck.

"Yes, it has." She smiled while resting an arm against

Dalvin's shoulder as he passed the blunt to her and propped himself against the front of the car. "Welcome home. I didn't think Greenwich would ever see you again. I thought the West Coast had claimed the Katri brothers."

"Nah, you know ain't no place like home."

"Damn right. Now, we can get money in a new era." Dalvin nodded. "This club is just the beginning. Let's go grab some food, baby, and head home." He removed himself from the car and stood but pointedly kept his arm around Noemi.

Dalvin and I grew up together, and everybody around the way knew me and Noemi fucked around heavy at one point. It wasn't no thang to me, though. Shit was in the past, and I wasn't looking to revisit. Seeing her did bring back some shit, but nothing I couldn't shake. Noemi was a couple of years older than me, but I lost my virginity to her. She taught me all about how to please a woman. I credit a lot of that to her because she had no problem showing and telling a nigga how to do some shit. We had some good times together, fucking up furniture and headboards. Shit, even now, a nigga caught a couple of flashbacks, and given how she was eye fucking me while hugged up under her man, she was reminiscing too.

"Y'all be easy." Spinning on the heel of my Alexander McQueen kicks, I headed to the back entrance of the building and let myself inside.

The smell of paint and sawdust hit me as soon as I entered. The furniture and bar were covered by white sheets, there were cans of paint, piles of wood, and scraps scattered about as well. They seemed to be making some progress from the last time I was there. I decided to go upstairs to where the offices were set up. There was one for D and one for me with two separate bathrooms as well. Both had glass windows behind our desks that viewed the entire club, and, of course, were bulletproof.

Strolling up the steps, I dug my cell out of my pocket to

shoot Lishan a text. Baby was asleep when I left, but I wanted her to know she was on my mind. I was putting in an effort, and I needed her to see that. Shit might have gone left, and I misjudged her, but I was on some different time now, and all that mattered was making sure she was straight. She had heart and little did she know I admired her more now than I ever thought I could.

The sun was coming up by the time the construction workers were walking out of the building. Once I locked up after everyone, I got in my whip and pushed it back to the house. Blowing another blunt with some classic E-40 slapping, I pushed it down the block of my street and hit the button to open the garage so I could slide in. Lately, it was really like coming home. I had a family in this mothafucka, and I didn't play about any of them, even Misael's grumpy ass.

It was almost seven thirty when I walked into my bedroom and found Lishan spread across the middle, curled up with one thigh out of the covers, and the rest of her shielded. Her locs were pulled back and tied into a scarf. Shorty looked peaceful as hell. I pulled my shirt over my head and went to take a quick shower before sliding in behind her and pulling her warm, soft curves against me. My hand landed on her stomach as I pressed my lips against her shoulder.

"Wood," Lishan whispered.

"What's on your mind, shorty?"

"Thank you for taking care of us. I honestly don't know what I would do right now if I didn't have you. If *we* didn't have you." She sniffled.

I propped my head up to check her out in the darkened room, illuminated by just a motion light from outside the window peeking through the crack of the blinds.

"Yo, you crying?"

"No." She quickly wiped her face.

Chuckling against her shoulder, I extended my arm to reach for hers, intertwining one of our hands together and observing how our skin complemented each other.

"I'm your sanctuary, shorty. Don't let that get you fucked up. I'll probably piss you off a lot, and I talk a lot of shit, but you ain't ever gon' find a nigga that goes harder for you than me."

"I have never been scared of you, Wood. I didn't expect anything from you in the beginning. I just knew the chemistry was there. I had no idea what it would grow into. I had fun with you. There were no expectations, and that scared me more than anything. I've peeped you over the last few months, and I questioned whether this was really what you wanted, and last night you made me see that there has been a change in you. I can't deny that or say that you haven't put in the effort. I just hope I'm worthy of it." She whispered that last part, and I pressed into her as my dick throbbed in anticipation.

I had never been one to deprive myself of pussy. Practicing self-control with Lishan this last month had been one of the hardest things I ever had to do. Now that I was this close to her, and she was naturally gorgeous as her chest nervously heaved, I couldn't help myself as she flipped over onto her back. Her nipples were like two pebbles poking through the thin material of the shirt she wore.

Taking my thumb, I toyed with one of them while planting a soft kiss on her lips that intensified within seconds. Her mouth was minty as I pulled back, a visage of thirst burning behind my stare. I soaked in every innocent feature of her face. Lishan had seen the ugliness of life up close, yet she was one of the prettiest women in the world.

"Don't ever question that. If I didn't know before, I'm locked in now." My lips latched onto hers while grabbing a handful of ass.

Our kisses heightened everything as her arms clutched

mine, and she locked me between her legs after prying them apart for me. She extended an arm, grabbing my rod in her hand and stroking him as a soft moan escaped her plush lips. Placing kisses all over her neck and collar bone, I sat up and helped her out of her shirt. Her curves were crazy, and her glistening bud had me salivating as I pulled my own shirt over my head and tossed it. Thumbing her nubbin, I knelt so I was face to face with her fat twat before fastening my mouth to it and sucking on it. Shorty bucked on the bed as her knees quivered, and I circled my tongue while pulling on her nub at the same time, which drove her crazy as she rocked on the bed.

"Shit! Wood! Baby... mmm..." Her satisfied moans echoed off the walls as I brought her to her peak, and she let go of a fat nut on my tongue.

Licking her folds, I stuck a finger inside, then another, and peered up to catch her reaction. The sex faces she made had me on brick as she trembled and bit her bottom lip to keep from screaming. She was so fucking wet that my hand was drenched when I pulled it out and aligned myself with her on the bed. Her warm center was waiting as I guided the tip of my dick toward it.

When I tapped at her opening, she spread her legs wider and licked her lips as I dipped inside her snug tunnel. Shit was gripping me so tight I almost fucking squealed like a bitch. Grabbing her thighs, I gave long strokes while watching my shit disappear, each time coming out with more of her sweet juices drenching it.

"Wood!" Her moans and those faces along with the sweat beads gathering on her chest had me on go.

I was tapping for gold, trying to make sure she came again because that wetness was life as I plunged further into her jewel. Cupping one of her breasts, I reached down to finger her berry like nipples at the same time as my strokes hit her bottom.

Her pussy was soaking, and she started leaking all over the fucking bed sheets as I went harder.

"Damn, Lis, this shit good, shorty! I need you to bust on this shit again, baby," I talked to her as I pressed my firm chest against her hard nipples and rocked in and out of her.

"You gon' do that for me?" I growled against her earlobe as her body shook. "Yeah, just like that." I sped up until my nuts dropped and my seeds spilled into her.

Covering her mouth in a kiss soaked with passion, I moaned against her lips until my dick became flaccid, and I slipped out of her. Turning on her side, she hooked her arms through mine and pulled herself into my chest as we caught our breath. Resting on my back, with my eyes on the ceiling, I could feel sleep ready to carry me away after that. Lishan traced my chest with her fingers and stared off as I draped an arm behind her back and kissed the top of her head.

"I don't know how you can be so chill about everything." She lifted her head and rested her chin against her hand, which was positioned on my chest. "You one of the calmest people I know, even when you're mad."

"My moms used to say that shit all the time." I chuckled. "Wylde is the one who flies off the handle, even though he comes off as cool and collected. When that nigga gets mad, watch out."

"What was your mama like? She had to be a hell of a woman to have two sons like you and him."

"She was my best friend. I could talk to her about anything. Literally. She talked hella shit too. I guess with a husband and two sons like us, it was a given." Thinking of my mother's gorgeous face had my chest tightening.

I hated that she died, but I knew she was in pain every single day while she was battling cancer. She wasn't here in the physical, but I always felt like she was watching over me and bro. It was the reason we came back to Greenwich to begin with because she thought it was where we belonged. She lived on the West Coast for Pops because that was what he wanted, and she would do anything to keep him happy.

"You don't talk too much about your family. Is there a reason behind that?" Lishan queried.

"I don't know. Wylde gets triggered about Moms. Nigga got a lot of internal issues where our parents are concerned. Oldest child syndrome and shit. They molded that nigga into the head-case he is today." I fisted some of my beard and reached for the blunt in the ashtray by the bed.

I was a smoker, so I usually had something within reach to fire up just out of habit. Placing the blunt between my lips, I also grabbed the BIC and sparked it.

"I didn't think Wylde was that bad."

"Nah, he just got a vice for bad bitches. Like our father. I get it. Ain't nothing like some pussy, that's for sure. Wylde also got Mommy issues, though. She accepted a lot of shit from our father, and he watched her go through it before I was born and after. It was shit that was kept on the low. Bitches weren't disrespectful or nothing like that, but our mother knew good and well that Waker was keeping company with anyone who would give him the time. She was at home sick and going through it, and she never stood up for herself. We didn't even hear them argue. When pops came home, he loved on her like he always did. That was one thing he stood on, showing her affection and making sure he was present when he was with her. The sicker she got, the less time he spent with her, though. I think it was hard for him to see her withering away like that. Wylde was pissed, though. He would go off, and him and Pops butted heads often over it. He wasn't even there when she took her last breath. I don't think my brother has ever forgiven him for that."

"Damn. I mean, it sounds like he has his reasons for it. I

believe he truly loves Shayne, though. I don't know. Seeing them together is just... I know I'm in the presence of something special when I see them look at each other. To them, it's like the rest of us are just there. Now, knowing all that Shayne has gone through, and hearing your take on Wylde, it sounds like they needed each other."

Inhaling the weed, I held it in my lungs and lifted my chin to exhale into the air.

"You pretty wise too, shorty. I can see the way you handle the kids from day to day that you are also very capable. You just had a missing piece. Me. But I'm here. I ain't here to make shit hard. You've had enough of that. Time for that soft girl era or whatever."

"You are something else, Woodrow Katri. I don't know what I'm going to do with you."

"Shit, fuck me good, cook, keep the house clean, and love on everybody around this mothafucka. We all need that. You do that shit effortlessly, whether a mothafucka want it or not."

"Yeah. You fought it long enough." She tittered, nipping at her bottom lip cutely.

Shit was the sweetest fucking thing. Usually, it meant she was horny and wanted more pipe. If that was the case, she was in store for another round before I tapped out and got some sleep. Mushing our lips together, I eased my tongue into her mouth and put the blunt out in the ashtray. Shorty came alive on top of me, and I admired her swollen clit and ample titties as she grabbed my stiff dick and slid him back into the place I now considered home.

"Fuck, Lis," I groaned, hands falling onto her silky skin as I sank my fingers into her thighs and rocked further inside of her until she was on the base of my shit with her hands against my chest, throwing her head back in bliss. A nigga loved that view.

Chapter 6
Shayne

A couple of days later...

For the last few nights, restlessness held me hostage. Any attempt I made to lie down was refuted by my own imagination. When I managed to fall asleep, it was brief and usually ended with me being rocked awake by Elim's face or Caterina's, and I would be steeped like a teabag in my own sweat. The kids were great and more than happy to be home. Nael kept an eye on them most of the time, and I rarely escaped my room.

During the day, it was okay. I could catch a nap and zone out, but it had to be pitch black in my room to do so. I was so jittery that it was giving me crackhead vibes that I couldn't shake. Oddly enough, when the sun went down is when I grew anxious and more irritable.

My nervous system resembled a motherboard with a bunch of lights going crazy, and I was afraid I was going to crash at any moment. I didn't even want to leave the house or be around people. Wylde gave me my phone back, but I hadn't turned it on, and I didn't want to take any calls. It was almost 5:00 a.m., and I'd been pacing for at least an hour. He was in bed sleeping so peacefully that watching him almost put me at ease. I had gone downstairs to make myself something to eat, thinking that would help settle me, yet there I stood at the doors to the balcony, looking into the backyard as the moon glowed against the navy sky.

"What are you doing?" Wylde asked in a groggy tenor that caused me to spin toward him as he sat up on one elbow, pinching the sleep from his eyes.

"Nothing. Go back to bed."

"What's wrong?" Shirtless, he sat up in bed and brought his knees up while wrapping his arms around them and locking his wrist with one hand.

"It's just hard to sleep sometimes. Especially at night."

"What do you need, mama?"

"Can you take us back? Back to before he came in and blew up our lives?" I questioned, eyes glimmering with tears I didn't want to drop.

I refused to give Elim that power. I didn't want to mention his name. If it ever came down to it, my children would block this man out of their memory. I knew it was easier said than done, considering he was their father, so that made him a part of them and part of their history. I wasn't going to be that kind of mother to deny them the truth. I was so pissed off that he could get to me like this. The nigga was dead and still held so much power.

"To before I even met him or allowed him into my life. He took everything from me!" Rage poured out of me in that last statement, and my tears were scorching hot when they fell against my face.

"Not everything," Wylde chimed in.

"You know what I've been thinking about the last three

days? Getting high. I've been locked up in here, physically aching from the withdrawals. I can barely eat. When I do, it all comes right back up. My body is rejecting everything. I just want to sleep, and when I do, he's there too. It makes me want to get high even more to cope. So, on top of everything else, I'm doing everything I can not to fall off this fucking wagon addicts always talk about. I'm a fucking addict, Wylde! If it wasn't for —" I almost let another truth slip off my lips but quickly zipped them closed as he listened attentively while giving me a peculiar glance.

Finally nodding along before swiping his hand along his five o' clock shadow, he seemed to mull over what I had just told him.

"And now I look weak. Like I can't fight this shit! Honestly... I don't know if I can," I whispered, shivering from the goosebumps that had popped up all over my flesh.

Tossing the covers from his legs, Wylde planted his feet on the floor on my side of the bed, and in nothing but his joggers, he towered over me. Canvassing his sculpted chest, decorated in various tattoos that reflected chapters of his life, I admired him. Things were better, but at the same time, we both seemed to be moving on eggshells, trying not to set the other off.

"You've been here for days, making sure I'm okay. I'm sure you have other things to do, Wylde."

"Nothing more important than making sure you're good."

"I want to fall apart right now. That's what I want, but I know I can't because I can't allow San and Storm to see me like that. I spent all that time not knowing what day it was and not being able to spend any time with them while Elim held us all hostage. They locked my babies in their rooms for hours. There was nothing I could do for any of us. He would come to my room and..." The air in my lungs was suddenly robbed.

Kneeling and clutching my stomach as stabbing pains filled it, I doubled over and wept as my knees fell into the carpet.

"Shayne—" Wylde tried to draw me in, but in that moment, I couldn't separate his touch from Elim's.

Flashbacks of him invading my body, forcing me to suck his dick, and any other fantasy he might have had while keeping me prisoner sent me spiraling into darkness as I shut my eyes. Scooting away from Wylde, I pressed my back into the wall next to my bedside table.

"No!" I shook my head and sucked in a deep breath.

Alarm filled his eyes as they raked over me while I shook so hard that I began to rock. My stomach might as well have been pitted out, but there was this rumbling underneath that was forcing the contents inside up into my throat. Leaping from the floor, I raced past Wylde into the bathroom and fell over the toilet just in time. Hugging the seat, I kept my head draped over the side while catching my breath. With the back of my hand, I wiped the side of my mouth.

I had hit rock bottom. Before, when I was running for my life, I thought that was it. This was a new low. Disgusted with myself, I reached up to flush the toilet and curled into a fetal position on the cold tile. It wasn't just the withdrawals kicking my ass, this baby was too. My hands were clammy, and the night shirt I wore was now sticking to my chest as my hair clung to the beads developing on my forehead.

"Tell me what you need, ma." Wylde's thick fingers grazed my scalp and lulled me into a calmer state.

Sniffling, I sucked in a few deep breaths and slowly began to sit up. Barely able to make him out through the glossiness of my eyes, I searched his handsome face. I had damn sure missed seeing it. My imagination just didn't seem to do the trick or provide the peace that his presence brought. He was my safety net. Laughing, I peered down at my distraught state.

"Right now, I could use a shower. Maybe I just need to get out of the house for a bit. I was contained for so long, some fresh air might do me and the kids some good. We could get breakfast and take them to the park. If you don't have anything to do, I want to go see Lishan too. I've been back a few days now."

"Say less. Come on." Wylde gave me his hand to take.

Pulling me up into his arms, he pinned me there and swept some of my hair from my damp face.

"You a soldier, Shayne. You will get through this too. Might not seem like it right now, but you will. I'm gon' make sure of it. I feel like I fucked up. A big part of me believed what I saw when I came to the house, and you were with him. It was easier to digest that you were just another woman out here scheming and playing on the affections of a man. Especially after I heard what they were saying about you. Everything told me when I went to see you that something was wrong. I just knew I couldn't move irrationally. A nigga's ego was bruised. So, I left. That ain't how a man moves."

"I'm glad you left," I whispered, watching his eyes as his brows furrowed. "What I mean is, Elim was crazy, impulsive, and deranged. He let his mama fill his head with some bullshit, and his daddy was never around to correct it. He had already killed my mother and my brother. My father is lying in a long-term care facility because of him. My worst fear was that he would do you and Wood, or anyone else who tried to help, the same way. I couldn't stomach that."

"You the kind of woman that you don't come across everyday. Selfless, thoughtful, and strong as hell. You have fought against everything that was sent to break you, Shayne."

"Sometimes I wonder if all the casualties in this war were worth it," I muttered. "My parents, my brother. Even San and

Storm. How do I rebuild the relationship with my children? I subjected them to—"

"First of all, don't take all the blame and carry it on your shoulders." Wylde was stern when he spoke as he cupped my chin and tilted my head toward him. "You were not alone in that. Their father was a narcissistic, abusive, controlling son of a bitch who didn't know what he had in you. He didn't deserve you or them. You ain't about to sit around here carrying that burden because, at the end of the day, you are a dope ass mother. Those kids love the shit out of you. Storm was worried about you the entire time. She cried, San comforted her, and I could see that even he was concerned."

"He pulled a gun on him. San was trying to step up for me, and his father pulled a gun on him. He's nine years old! What the fuck is that? Thank God Storm got away when she did and got to a phone. She was so brave. She didn't care that Caterina was using her as a punching bag; she just knew she had to do something."

"Sounds like she is as smart and resourceful as her mama," Wylde replied as a small smirk danced across his lips. "And I know I made the right decision when I pulled that trigger."

'This could all blow back on us, Wylde," I warned.

"And I'll be ready for it," he assured, pressing his warm, supple lips against mine.

He ran a hot shower for me, which I immediately climbed into. For at least twenty minutes, I let the water wash over me. I had to get back to me. To the life I was starting to envision for me and my children. Once I was dressed in black tights, a pair of black and white Nike dunks, with a black and white logo shirt, I went to my closet to dig the black and white letterman jacket out. A bitch felt like she was in mourning or something. The weather was shifting again, so I knew that spring was now

battling with winter to come out on top. Either way, I ne
be in dress code.

After pulling my hair into a messy bun up top, I g
my cell and trotted toward the bedroom door. The
laughter coming from the kids, and it was melodic. As I
the bottom of the staircase, my phone vibrated in my har
I saw that it was a text from Lishan.

*Lishan: We need to get together. I am going crazy an
some ADULT time. And girl time.*

Me: Great minds think alike. I'll be by after breakfast.

Storm and Santana were seated around the island
Nael had just brought his mug to his lips to take a sip
coffee when I appeared in the doorway. Pausing, a fa
twinkle lit up his eyes as he soaked me in. Behind him, \
was pouring his own cup, still in his pajamas.

"Well, look at you. You almost look normal. You go
light around you."

Wylde's eyes caught mine, and I quickly turned awa
focused on the kids. I couldn't do this right now. It was
enough trying to push through the damn day and not get
despite being pregnant. I knew once I spilled that tru
whole other set of questions would follow. I already knew
was what. I just didn't want him to question it.

"Probably from all the vomiting I have been doing," I j
while approaching the counter.

I greeted San with a hug first as he peered into his bo
oatmeal. Storm was perky beside him as she scooped hers
her mouth.

"What's wrong?" I pried, throwing an arm over his sh
ders and searching his pensive face.

"Nothing."

"He came and slept in my room with me last night.
slept on the floor," Storm informed everyone present.

"Why did you do that, San?"

"I just wanted to make sure she was good." He nodded.

"You said it was because you had bad dreams and couldn't sleep," Storm corrected as he cut a warning glare in her direction.

My baby turned her nose and lip up at him as he caught an attitude. She didn't think she had said anything wrong.

"I said that between us, Storm, dang."

"San, it's okay." Grabbing his chin, I forced him to face me.

His usually warm chestnut eyes were so downcast. My baby boy had seen the ugliness of the world up close, and now he was changed. Damn Elim for robbing him of his innonence like that.

"Hey. It's okay. I have them too. It makes me not want to go to sleep."

"Is that why you always up all night, walking around and checking everything?" he queried.

"You hear me?"

"I see you when you come in my room and make sure all the windows are locked," my son confessed.

"San—"

"Wylde said I was supposed to protect you. You and Storm. I didn't do that." His head sank in defeat, and my eyes filled to the brim with fresh tears.

I pulled him into a hug, and my eyes met Wylde's as he stopped at the counter. This was the shit I hated. The awful position that Elim had put me in was unfair. He got to be the ain't shit parent and live his life, while I was left with the brunt of everything else.

"San, you are nine years old, son. What can you really do? You did what you were supposed to do. I'm your mother. I failed you, baby. I didn't do everything I could to make sure you

and Storm were okay." Pulling back, I peered into his broken face.

I was glad that I didn't look at either of my babies and see their father. In my mind, they resembled me, from their wide set eyes, to the perfect Rogan nose that I inherited from my own parents.

"He was a bad man. His mama was too." Storm took a bite of her oatmeal and both of her little brows knitted into the cutest little scowl.

She had the right name because my baby girl was going to be a force.

"I agree. They are out of our lives. Now, we pick up the pieces and try to move on. It won't be easy, but... it's what we have to do." I put an arm across both of them and kissed the top of their heads. "Finish eating. I am dying to get out of this house."

"Mind if this old man tags along? I got no plans for the day, and I told the kids I wouldn't be far," Nael requested.

"Is that what this is, or you working another angle, old man?" Squinting, I caught Nael red handed, and he lightly shrugged.

"I can be concerned and want to be close, right?"

"Yeah. You can." Snickering, I shook my head as Wylde brought two cups of coffee to the counter and slid one in front of me.

"For you, with a pound of sugar and all the cream," he jested before bringing his cup to his lips.

Usually, I was a fanatic for the stuff and had to have it at least twice a day. He knew my habits because he had both lived and worked with me to witness it. Today I wasn't feeling it, and I knew on top of that with this pregnancy, it probably just wasn't a good look. Screw might have said everything was okay with this baby, but I was fucked up for the first seven weeks of this shit, so I couldn't be too careful.

"Thanks, but I'm good."

"You good on coffee?" Nael interjected. "Sounds like blasphemy to me." He brought his cup to his lips for another sip.

"I'm going to make sure the kids are good and do something to Storm's wild hair."

Within the next thirty minutes, we were all piling into Wylde's truck and taking off. The day was nice. The sun glowed in the sky. It was a little cloudy, and there was still a slight chill in the air, but not enough to cripple you or force you into multiple layers. We stopped at Smoothie King and grabbed a few drinks for everyone before Wylde took us to a park near the house he shared with Wood. Nael got out with Storm and San as they went to explore the park. Wylde had us posted near the trashcans with a clear view of them. We weren't parked more than a few steps away as Storm ran to the swings and San went to the monkey bars. Since they were all out of the car, Wylde sparked his blunt and took a couple of tokes before passing to me.

"It's just weed," he said. "It might make you feel better. I personally don't consider it a drug like all the other shit. I've done my research. Even thinking of investing in a dispensary."

I grabbed the blunt and took a puff. As the THC went through me, I almost immediately felt better off the taste alone. After a couple more hits, I sent it back to Wylde and stared out my window as San and Storm had a ball with Nael and some of the other kids on the playground. Wylde's phone rang, but instead of answering, he checked the display and sent them to voicemail.

"How are things at the office? I told you if you need to be somewhere—"

"I'm where I want to be, and where I need to be. That other

shit can wait." He leaned across the middle console and reached for my hand. "I want you to focus on taking the good shit with the bad in life. Look at that." He nodded to where Storm and San were laughing their asses off with Nael. It was a beautiful moment. "Worry about that. Keep them smiling and laughing, reminding them that bad shit does happen, but you can always push through."

My heart fluttered. This man. He had no idea the kind of gift he was. Sniffling, I lowered my head as my fingers fidgeted with one another.

"Since the day we met, you've been dropping nothing but gems for me, Wylde. You encourage me, you provide for me, and I don't expect any of that."

"I do it because it's what you deserve, Shayne. It's pretty simple, mama. From the moment I looked into your eyes, I knew you were worth it." Intensity brewed between us, and our fingers interlocked before our mouths hungrily attacked each other in a heated kiss.

This was the kind of kiss that led to more, but, of course, we were not in any position to give in to that in that moment. Grabbing some of his beard that had grown out, I gave short pecks to his full lips before retreating. The kids played for another thirty minutes or so before we loaded up and headed toward the house to see Wood, Lishan, and her family.

Wylde pulled up the elevated driveway and parked. The neighborhood was so still as we all climbed out of the car. The kids ran ahead of us to the door. Storm was anxious to ring the doorbell. When it flung open, Lishan appeared, dressed down in a Pink two piece sweatsuit and a pair of slides. With her locs pulled away from her face at the top, they hung down her back as she greeted my kids with the biggest grin and open arms.

"Hey, Lishan!" Storm gave her a warm hug before racing past her.

"What's up, San? I know it hasn't been that long, but you look bigger than when I last saw you." Their hug was brief as my son stepped past her.

The minute she saw me, she came trotting out of the house to welcome me.

"You. I am so glad to see you!" My chest nearly cracked from her genuine warmth while embracing me.

I didn't realize I needed it when she pulled back to get a good look at me.

"You okay?"

"One day at a time." I forced a smile through my tears, and she nodded. "Well, come inside. Meet everyone. I told them all about you, and I can't wait 'til all my favorite people meet." Lishan threw an arm over my shoulders and walked me up the sidewalk to the house.

Once we were inside, I found her siblings all lingering in the doorway from the living room just a few steps to our right. The arched doorway gave a view of the vast space. Everything was neutral around there. The setting wasn't too masculine or feminine, but it was classic; elegant.

"Ledger, Lincoln, and Lumiere, this is Shayne. These are her two kids, Santana and Storm, and y'all already know Uncle Wylde." She waved him off casually as he closed and locked the door.

"Hi." They responded in unison as Nael came up beside me.

"Who is he?" her little sister, Lumiere questioned as a noise jarred my attention in the opposite direction.

Coming down the hall was a man in a wheelchair, and he was rather slow. With oxygen tubes up his nose, he stopped just beside me and the kids.

"This is my uncle, Nael," I introduced everyone.

"And this is Misael, my grandpa." Lishan turned and rested a hand on his shoulder.

"Hello. Nice to meet you," I addressed him with a wave.

He made some grumbling noises, but that was it as his gaze drifted past me onto Nael. Shit was weird, but the way they sized each other up, you would have thought they had known each other once upon a time or something. I brushed it off and went into the living room, peeling out of my jacket and tossing it on the back of a large pedestal type chair with fancy lettering in the print. It resembled a postcard to me with the intricate details of the script.

"Where's Wood?"

"Downstairs in the basement. He had some work stuff to take care of," Lishan replied. "You want something to eat? It's all I seem to do lately." She gave an eyeroll, and I trailed her through the house to the open kitchen.

The kids, all but Ledger, had already raced upstairs to the bedrooms and were paying us no mind. I think they were just glad to have someone to play with.

"I need something sweet. You got cookies, or a pie? Some German chocolate cake sounds amazing." I gushed from one side of the island as she gaped at me incredulously from the opposite.

"Who the fuck just got German chocolate cake sitting around they house, Shayne?" She turned her nose up, and I tittered.

"Obviously not yo' ass, Lishan." The weed had me a little calmer and pulled together as I plopped into a bar chair.

Clasping my hands together, I watched her go over to the fridge and pull out a roll of those Pillsbury cookies.

"Now, these, I do have."

"So, how are you?" I pried as she went to grab a knife and baking tray.

Shrugging, she rejoined me at the counter.

"I don't know. Just going with it. I'm not bad, but I'm not the greatest."

"I know that feeling." My gaze diverted as she cut into the roll of dough.

"I bet you do. I can't imagine what you've been through. What the kids have been through."

"It was rough. Not in the sense that we were living without amenities or anything like that. Emotionally, it was damaging as hell. Now I'm trying to figure out what happens now."

"Shayne, it's been like three days. You don't have to have all the answers and figure all this out now. Your entire life was turned upside down. You're allowed a little grace." She started to scoop the dough and make little balls before setting them aside on the ungreased tray.

"I'm anxious all the time. I can't shake the feeling that something else bad is just waiting to drop in the middle of my life. Who wants to live like that? What is wrong with me?" Hopping up from the stool, I began to pace the floor.

"You're traumatized and have PTSD from all the shit you've been through. Ain't nothing wrong with you."

"Oh, she's crazy as hell. That's a given." Wood strolled into the room with sarcasm.

"Fuck you!" I snapped and watched him grin like a Chesire cat.

"What I tell you?" I watched him ease up behind Lishan and hug her while planting kisses along her neck.

"She has been through a lot. She's got every reason to be guarded and on pins and needles the way she is. Hell, I get it."

"You get that, but what you not understanding is, you got me and Wylde in your lives now. We fuck up, but that won't stop us from doing everything in our power to make sure y'all good, whether you want it or not. Ain't no bitch in my blood,

Lis. Not a drop." He turned her head so he could capture her mouth with a sloppy kiss that had me blushing and turning my head just as Wylde's fine ass waltzed in.

Before he could utter a word, the doorbell chimed. Wood pulled away from Lishan and drew his pistol as he rounded the counter with Wylde not far behind. I knew we couldn't be too careful, and I loathed the idea of constantly living in fear or the edge of it for that matter. The voices were muffled, caused Lishan and I to throw a curious stares at each other as the front door slammed shut. Together, we strolled around the corner of the kitchen into the hallway with ceilings at least twenty feet tall.

The sight of Kaori was an instant trigger as she moved away from the older gentleman she strolled through the doors with and went to greet Wylde. Wood and the old man dapped each other before embracing, and it was evident from their expressions and the way they handled each other that they were familiar. Scrutinizing the gentleman, I swear I saw distinct traces of Wylde, Wood, and even Rich. When Wylde took a step back, Kaori reared her head. She appeared to be trying to welcome him with a kiss, which he was rejecting as his arms tucked over his buff chest.

"And who do we have here?" the older man asked, curious eyes raking over both Lishan and me as we also waited to be introduced.

"Shit, Pop, that's Lishan. I told you about her," Wood responded.

"You did. You didn't mention that she looked like a baby, though. Damn, girl, how old are you?"

"I'm almost twenty-one," Lishan spoke up.

"Hmm," was all he offered as he looked her up and down before his penetrating, cognac tinted orbs linked with mine.

She shot me a side eye, and I could tell off the rip that she was about to let that reckless mouth of hers go. Resting a hand on her arm, I tried to get her to take it down a notch.

"And you are?"

"Shayne," I responded.

"This is Waker Katri. Our father," Wylde acknowledged, taut with his hands in his pocket as he sized his father up with Kaori.

The resemblance was un fucking canny. Their bloodline was clearly strong. Waker was more reserved. I could see it from the glint that he masked behind his stare. His eyes spoke more words than his lips in the few minutes he had stood in front of me. I wasn't about to let him intimidate me in any way. I'd had enough of that to go around in my life. Even Kaori standing there all smug while Wylde wore guilt like a coat didn't shake me. I had gone through literal hell, so this shit was a cake walk, at least that's what I told myself.

"Nice to meet you." The tight smile on my face was all I could muster.

I might have been standing tall like everything was sweet, but that was far from the truth. The anxiety from earlier was creeping up, and I was doing my best not to go to that dark place today. Thinking of Wylde with another woman was enough to turn me up though.

"What is she doing here? Where have you been? Why aren't you answering my calls?" Kaori drilled him.

"Why don't we leave you alone and let you answer those questions," I muttered.

"Let's go make those cookies." Lishan pulled me along toward the kitchen.

She had saved the day because my adrenaline was about to kick in, and I wasn't trying to make that impression on Wylde's father off the rip. I'd heard very little of the man, and what I did know wasn't very impressive. It was no thing for me not to get along with a nigga's parents. Sometimes the shit wasn't meant to be, and I wasn't in the business of ass kissing.

Wylde

"Pop, what you doing here? And how did you end up with him?" I questioned as soon as Lishan and Shayne were out of earshot.

"I asked you a question too, Wylde. What is she doing here? I thought you were done with her? What the fuck is going on?" A hand flew to Kaori's hip as she huffed and puffed in my face.

Swiping my beard and shaking my head, I backed away from her.

"Some shit happened. It's a long story, and it's really nobody's business. She's here because I want her here, though."

"Is this where you have been the last few days?" Kaori's brows lifted as her mouth fell open. "With her?"

"Chill on the dramatics, aight. I was gon' hit you up. I just had a lot going on with her and the kids—"

"So, you dropped me without so much as a text or phone call... for a baby mama ass bitch who left you for another nigga?"

Kaori's inquiry sent my nostrils flaring because she was on some disrespectful shit.

"There was more to the story than that. I misunderstood. Now, I have all the facts."

"So that's it?" she screeched. "What about me, Wylde? What am I supposed to do with that?"

"You do what you want. I'm telling you what it is."

"That's pretty impulsive, son, to make a decision like that. You've known K for a long time..."

"You need to stay out of this." My forehead drew into a scowl.

"Your father has always been our biggest supporter, Wylde. After your mama died..." Kaori attempted the same shit she always did. Playing on our past was a part of her scheme. She used that shit like a weapon every single time, and the shit was getting old.

"We not doing this."

"And you don't get to choose another bitch and just walk away from me... again!" Kaori spat.

"You need to calm the fuck down. There are kids around here."

"Oh, I don't give a fuck!" Her eyes bucked wildly.

"K." My father's hands fell on her shoulders, and oddly enough, she relaxed under his touch.

"Talk to him, Waker. Talk some sense into him."

Spinning on the heel of her red bottoms, she stomped toward the door, shoes clicking with each step. After she stormed outside like a fucking toddler, my father faced me.

"What are you doing, Wylde?"

"I asked you to stay out of this, Pop. This ain't your business. What you doing being all buddy buddy with her for anyway? We broke up a long time ago."

"Kaori is family. Ever since Kaitlyn died, I promised to be there for her. You and your brother did too. What happened to that?"

"You act like she's this thing that needs to be taken care of. She's pretty fucking capable, and it ain't my responsibility to make sure she straight all the fucking days of her life," I argued.

"Then why invite her back into your life if you were just going to play with her?"

"That's not what it was. You should recognize it. Drowning

your pain, masking the hurt with whatever feels good. You familiar with that, right Pop?" My line of questioning sent guilt flickering across his expression. "The difference is, I've learned from my mistakes. At first, when K came back, I wondered what could have been. When I got a taste of life without Shayne, and those kids, that shit changed my perspective. I decided to not be the selfish man I always saw represented. Unlike you, I don't want to ever hurt or disappoint her because she looks to me to make life better for her."

"You think it's that easy? You have no fucking idea, son!"

"What I know is, I don't want to be like you. I don't want to wake up someday and have children who resent me or blame me for all the hurt I caused their mother that they had to witness."

"Yeah? Well, newsflash, those ain't your children, and she's barely your fucking woman from what I hear."

Glancing past Waker, I caught Wood running his fingers through his sponge top and bowing his head in admission. When it came to our father, he was known to gossip like a bitch. I hated that he felt the need to keep him informed on my life, but the nigga never wanted to reach out to me personally. Ol' sit by the sidelines ass nigga.

"It ain't about that, and you too old not to get it. You ain't never been the selfless type, though, Pop. So, I don't expect that from you," I pointed out.

"Wylde—" Wood made an attempt to intervene.

"Nah, let him talk. Since he's reformed now and all that other shit. Let me see you hold down a family, a wife, and children, and not lose yourself in it. You all self-righteous with me because you upset with how your mama allowed herself to be treated."

My anger sprang out like a jack in the box, causing me to snatch him up and slam him into the nearest wall before I got in his face, arranging my features in a grimace when I addressed him.

"Don't you ever speak on her again after what you did! You don't get to! It wasn't my responsibility to be there for her in sickness and in health. That was you! Soon as it got real, your punk ass couldn't take it."

"And you hate to be reminded that you are just like me." The smugness dancing across his face caused my fist to lift and jam right into his jaw.

"Fuck you!" I spat in his face.

"I'm still your father. You better release me, Wylde, before I show you why I'm not to be fucked with."

"Wylde, fall back." Wood's hands pulling on my shoulder was the only thing sparing me from beating our father's ass.

His youngest son was his saving grace, because I was about to mop the entire foyer with him.

"I'm going to get some air." Marching past both my father and brother after releasing him, I stormed out the front door and slammed it shut behind me.

Waker was an automatic trigger for me, taking me outside of myself as I paced the porch of the house and replayed the conversation we'd just had. He couldn't fathom where I was coming from. A large part of me believed he never loved my mother like he said he did, or he would have been at her side when she took her last breath instead of somewhere more than likely laid up with the next bitch. I could never picture doing no shit like that to someone I claimed to love.

I noticed the rental that Kaori had been driving parked on the curb, which meant she was still lurking. I was low key irritated as hell that my father thought it was cool to show up with her like that. I had made it clear to her that we were just fucking, and I wasn't interested in anything else, despite our past. It wasn't just about Shayne. We were two different people now.

Kaori did a lot of travel for work, her and her girls went on excursions, and she was living her best single life. She wanted me to join her in traveling the world and all that other shit. Maybe when we were younger, that might have appealed to me, but a nigga was over thirty and looking for more in life than that now. She could be fulfilled with those things, but now that I had a life with Shayne and the kids, it showed me that there was damn sure more to the world than that.

"Wylde." She slammed her car door shut and started back up the sidewalk to the porch where I stood.

"You need to bounce. I don't have time for you or your fucking tantrums. You knew what this shit was. I didn't force you to stick around or guarantee anything other than a spot in my bed occasionally when a nigga needed it."

"So, you used me?"

"You used me too. You wanted it just as much as I did, and it ain't my fault if you were willing to settle for it, knowing I wasn't offering anything else," I verbalized.

"How can you be so cold with me of all people? Who was there for you when your mother died—"

"And you can stop throwing that shit in my face!" I growled, jumping off the porch and in her face, causing her to reel back cowardly.

"I—"

"You think because you were a part of my life back then that it entitles you to a place in it now. It doesn't." My words caused her eyes to flicker with fresh tears.

Rarely did Kaori ever display hurt or any emotion other than rage or a pout.

"I don't understand you."

"You not stupid, ma. We been here before. We were two different people then, and we are now. Ain't no reason to be dragging this out."

"Oh, but it is. I know the outcome, Wylde, because you are just like me. You're selfish, you're adventurous, and we always know how to make each other feel good. You are flawed, baby. You think this is going to work with this bitch and her kids? Why? Because you've changed?" she teased, inching closer and closing the small space left between us with her soft body. "That's a lie, and we both know it. If you had changed, I wouldn't have been in your bed the entire time this girl was gone. If you were so devoted to her, why come back to me in the first place?" She toyed with the collar of my shirt, and the door behind us creaked, letting me know that someone else had joined in our conversation.

The taunting smile on Kaori's face informed me it was exactly who I thought it was. When I pivoted around, Shayne stood on the porch, arms crossed over her full breasts as she soaked me in with my ex.

"I would love to know the answer to that myself."

"The truth is, Wylde never stopped loving me or wanting me. Even through his relationship with Billie, we would randomly link for a weekend in some foreign, romantic city and enjoy each other. We lost our virginity to each other. That kind of bond doesn't just go away."

"K, shut the fuck up." I gritted my teeth, and she simpered smugly at Shayne.

"She might as well know now what she's in for, right? I mean, women come and go from your life, Wylde. Not everyone sticks," she emphasized while raking her dark, oval shaped orbs over Shayne.

"So, do you get like a badge of honor or something for being stupid or pathetic?" Shorty unfolded her arms as her brows furrowed so deep her forehead wrinkled, and she stepped off the porch into Kaori's space.

"Bitch, you want to talk pathetic? What kind of man wants

to play stepdaddy to a bitch and her two brats? You think he really gives a fuck about you—"

"If he didn't, you wouldn't be so bothered." Shayne shrugged, and I tried to hide my smile because she wasn't letting Kaori get under her skin.

The moment K swung, trying to connect with Shayne's face, shorty stepped up and rocked her with a two piece that sent her stumbling and eventually falling on her ass in the yard. Blood dripped from her nose down her chin, and Kaori brought a hand to the warm liquid on her face. Her eyes stretched like two big rubber bands when she saw all that red.

"Stupid hoe!" She was on her feet and about to rush Shayne when I positioned myself between them. With my back to Shayne, I held Kaori back as she lunged.

"Let the bitch go!" Shayne yelled.

"Get the fuck out of here, K!" I shoved her back so hard she almost lost her balance again as her wild eyes met mine.

"This is the last time you pick another bitch over me, Wylde! I swear to God, so you better make this choice and live with the fucking consequences!" she spat.

"I just did. Leave." I pointed to her car, and shock flitted across her face.

Spinning back toward Shayne, I placed a hand on the small of her back and led her back up the porch steps. Growling like a linebacker, Kaori charged at me, her fists landing on my back repeatedly as she lost her damn mind. Shayne circled around a nigga so swiftly I didn't have time to catch her as she yanked Kaori back by the thirty-inch wig and started to ram her fist into her face repeatedly.

"Bitch must be slow!" she declared between punches.

Kaori didn't stand a chance. Shayne was unleashing on her, and it was obvious everything from the last few months was a driving force behind her sudden rage. The door to the house flew open, and my pops, Wood, and Lishan came racing out to see what was unfolding.

"You just gon' let her do that to her, Wylde?" Waker asked as Shayne swung Kaori around and kicked her so hard she hit the concrete and remained curled up there.

She didn't let up. Shorty was kicking her while she was down, sending David Beckham blows to her stomach until Wood and I stepped up to pull her off her.

"The fuck, Wylde? That shit ain't right!" Waker rushed to Kaori and knelt.

She could barely move as she held her stomach and attempted to breathe as her face filled with anguish.

"Get her the fuck out of here!" I shoved Shayne toward the porch, and she stomped behind Lishan inside.

Wood remained out front with Pops, helping him get her to the rental. I slammed the door shut as Shayne spun on me with her wrath.

"Was that necessary?"

"You really want to go there with me right now?" she asked, still huffing and puffing as she took her ponytail down and ran her fingers through her hair.

The shit was kind of sexy, but I couldn't neglect the severity of the situation. The house was full of kids for one, and all of them had been subjected to one bullshit circumstance or another. I didn't want to have to worry about her when I wasn't around dog walking a mothafucka.

"You came at her like a rabid dog."

"And she deserved that shit! Oh, you want to go make sure she's okay? Is that what this is, Wylde? Was she right about everything?"

"Fuck nah. I just don't need you fighting battles for me."

"Oh, that wasn't for you." Shayne laughed like a

madwoman as she put her shoulder length hair back into a bun. "She earned that shit for talking about me like that."

"I didn't know yo' little ass had that in you." Lishan held a hand up, and Shayne high fived her just as Wood came through the front door, shaking his head.

"Damn, Shayne, you could have let her get one hit off."

Lishan and Shayne both fell over laughing, looking crazy as hell as me and bro side eyed each other. Yeah, it was official. They both had a few screws loose.

Wood decided to make a day of it, so he fired up the grill, and Lishan and Shayne prepared the sides while the kids ran from outside to inside and back again, having a ball. Nael and Misael spent a little time together, and then Misael went to take a nap since he was tired. Shayne's uncle remained in the living room, catching up on highlights and drinking beer while the rest of us did our thing. Shit seemed a little off to me, but I wasn't there to question it. The day had been eventful enough. Lishan went to take Wood a tray of marinated meat she had prepared, and Shayne remained at the counter, peeling the shells off the eggs for the potato salad.

"You sure you don't want a beer or a glass of wine? It's okay."

"Wylde, I'm fine. Please stop hovering over me." Rolling her eyes, she set an egg on a plate along with a few others that had already been peeled.

"I'm hovering because I care." I came up behind her on the other side and pressed my semi hard dick into her.

Instead of melting like she would in the past, she was tense as her shoulders rose and her breathing seemed to get caught in her chest. When I was close to her, she often flinched, and I hated that shit. Elim had really done a number on her, and I couldn't help but wonder how much he had inflicted on her. Something was off about Shayne since she woke up. It was in her eyes and the way she averted them from me when I looked at her most of the time. I was perceptive as a mothafucka on her, and she was putting up this shield trying to block it when I was trying to read her.

"I know. I'm fine. I don't need you checking on me every five minutes like a child."

"You can kill all that nonsense you talking about. You been through a lot. I'm always gon' be checking on you," I assured her.

My phone went off in my pocket with an alert. Curious, I pulled it out and studied the notification on the screen. Someone had sent me a personal message. Frowning, I opened the attachment, and a video immediately populated on my screen.

"The fuck?" I shook my head as Shayne stepped closer, so she could also see what was going on.

"Oh, my God, is that—"

"Shit!" I hissed as Lishan and Wood came strolling through the door, laughing together. The display of shock across me and Shayne's faces had them both pausing in their stride.

"Damn, what's wrong?" Lishan gave a screw face.

"Someone just sent me a video. Shit is going viral." I held up my phone and slid it across the counter to my brother.

He scooped it up immediately and took a peek. Someone had leaked some footage of Lishan. Shit was dated; I could tell by the resolution. She was smaller, but it was obvious that it was her from the way the camera zoomed in on her face. Wood's nostrils flared as he gripped my phone so tight, he almost broke it before placing it back on the counter.

"What is it?" Lishan queried, reaching for the phone.

"Don't look at that shit." Wood shook his head.

Ignoring him, she snatched the phone, and the smile she wore instantly fell with the rest of her face as she watched everything play out. With her mouth falling open in disbelief, her melanin skin was was robbed of all color. Lifting her eyes to search our faces, embarrassment and shame resided there now.

"Well, at least I know Merlin wasn't bluffing."

"Lis—" Wood gently placed a hand on her arm.

"No." Lishan shook her head and set my phone back on the counter. "It is what it is, Wood. Nothing I can do about it. The whole world is going to be able to see this or pull it up. There are no excuses. I need to talk to the kids about it. I don't want them to hear this from somewhere else or anything like that."

"Nobody can fault you for how you took care of yourself and your family, Lis. So, don't you dare let another mothafucka make you feel bad about it," Shayne piped up.

"I'm going to check on the kids." Sniffling with misting eyes, Lishan set the empty meat tray on the counter and walked off.

When she cleared the room, our eyes all linked at one point, and I could see that Wood was ready to spaz.

"I'm tired of playing with this mothafucka." He gritted his teeth as both of his hands rested against the counter.

"Tell me what you want to do." At the end of the day, I had my brother's front and back. However he wanted to move was fine with me. Merlin and his mama deserved every ounce of energy bro was ready to give them.

"Not right now. Let's eat and try to enjoy this day. Been enough shit going on. I just want to have one day where we can sit and act fucking normal."

"As normal as we can get," Shayne mumbled.

"Why don't you put some ice on that hand, Ali?" Wood kidded.

A couple of hours later, we were all in the kitchen with a large serving of food spread over the counters. The kids were all at the table eating, and Nael and Misael had joined them to keep them under control while the rest of us remained at the island together. Lishan and Shayne were side by side on bar chairs. Even though food was all she had been talking about since we'd been here, Lishan seemed to have lost her appetite as she moved food around on her plate. Shayne was easily mopping everything up in hefty portions, though, like she was starving.

Wood's fork clanked loudly against his plate when he dropped it. Lishan's somberness was getting to us both. She didn't deserve this, and it was obvious that despite the front she was trying to put up, that the shit bothered her on some level. Once we got everything cleaned up and the food put away, Shayne had to wrangle the kids, so we could leave. Storm and San were having a good time with Linc and Lumi. All of a sudden they were cousins. I thought the shit was dope as fuck though. Everybody needed a tribe. I understood that lonliness better than mothafuckas presumed.

"Hey, so I am thinking of going back to work next week. Not full time, just putting in a few hours to slowly ease back in. What do you think? You ready? I know you've been out on medical and everything." Shayne nudged Lishan's shoulder as we stood in the entryway.

"The doctor cleared me. I could use a distraction," she muttered with a shrug.

"Okay, well, I will let you know. Maybe we can just carpool or something."

"I don't know about all that," Wood chimed in.

"Wood, we can't sit around like ducks, waiting to be plucked off. I'm so tired of living like that." Shayne huffed.

"Me too. I know this might draw more attention to me, but so what? I can't run and hide."

"And I'm not going to let you." Shayne embraced her. "So, I will hit you up later."

I handed Shayne the keys, and Wood offered to walk them out while I went to grab the food we had packed to take with us. Nael and Misael were still in the kitchen since Lishan was near passing out in the living room on the couch, surrounded by her siblings.

"I guess it is a small world." Nael chuckled.

"Not small enough," Misael grumbled.

The conversation seemed personal, so instead of walking in to interrupt it, I lingered near the doorway with my back pressed against the wall.

"I'm not here to bring any problems, old man." Nael tittered and brought his arms into the air.

"Then you should leave and take your niece and her kids with you."

"What is wrong with you? What I do to you?"

"It's not about you. It's about Lishan and Shayne," Misael said.

"What about them?" Nael queried.

"I know it might have been a long time, but you ain't no fool. The last time you came around these parts, you were with your brother, Miles Rogan. Smooth ass playboy. The kind of nigga that seems harmless but can bring about all kinds of destruction if you let him," Misael ranted.

"Like you said, that was a long time ago. Me, Miles, Rich, and his brother all ran in the same circles. I'm not that same young boy, though, and I wasn't so bad to begin with. My niece and her children mean everything to me. Miles might as well be dead."

"So, I heard," Misael mumbled. "It's probably for the best."

"The fuck you say?" I had never heard that kind of animosity in Nael's voice before.

"Don't get all indignant with me. Your brother came here and smooth talked my daughter. He got her pregnant."

"Leslie had a baby?" Nael shrilled.

"Her name is Lishan Grey. You met her. You sat right here with her, talking and laughing like everything was all good." Misael began to cough.

"Wait, are you saying that... that girl, is she Mile's daughter?" Nael queried, disbelief lacing his tone.

"That's exactly who she is. Which makes her Shayne's little sister."

Nothing but alarms began to ring as the news rocked my brain. *What the fuck was going on?* This was the last thing I expected to hear, and I couldn't just ignore it, could I? Swiping my hand down my face, I tried to shake off the news and appear normal as I stepped into the room. Both men were caught off guard and tightened up in my presence.

"Shayne and the kids are loading up. I came to get the food," I announced, which caused Nael to squint as Misael gnawed his gums together like he often did.

"I guess I'll be heading out. Nice to meet you." Nael waved to Misael on his way to the door, and I went to grab the food containers from the table.

"Take it easy tonight, old man."

"Mmm hmm." His dark eyes penetrated me.

Shaking my head, I strolled toward the door, arms full of to go dishes. I could tell the wheels were moving in his head, and he was wondering what I'd heard. Misael might have been terminally ill, but he wasn't slow by any means. I had spent enough time around him over the last month or so to know that. He was very observant, and on his good days, he could still keep up. The doctors were projecting maybe another six months or so for him to live. Lishan got points from me for being a real one for her family. Shorty might have been young, but she had a heart of gold. She had become like a little sister to me. So in my eyes, Merlin's bitch ass deserved to taste the dirt. It was time for me and Wood to put in that work.

"Lis!" I called out, causing her to pop her head up on the couch from zoning out on the TV.

"Keep yo' head up, sis!"

"Goodnight, Wylde." With her hand propped into her hand she gave me a half smile.

"Shit, you need the help at the office, right? Shayne is one of our top agents. We doubling up security and getting both her and Lis tracking devices," Wood suggested.

"How the fuck we gon' manage that? She ain't going for that shit," I argued.

"She ain't got to. I got a homie that can put a piece in any item of jewelry. So, pick out a bracelet, necklace, or something she will always want to wear. I'm doing the same for Lishan. Have it to me in the next day or two."

"Aight. I think I already got something. What you think about Pop showing up?"

"I don't know. He didn't mention the shit to me. I don't know what's going on," Wood replied.

"He needs to take his ass back home before I beat his ass across the fucking country."

"Bro, you need to relax." He placed a hand on my shoulder.

"How the fuck we supposed to do that, Wood?"

"Go home. Chill with your girl and those kids. They need you, and you need they asses too, quiet as it's kept. We can talk shop tomorrow."

He knew that shit was easier said than done. I loved my mother more than any other woman on earth. When she died, a large part of me was taken with her. I moved on, and never properly grieved, and my father was a huge trigger for me. The way he was so careless with her heart, with her fucking life, made me sick. It was better when he was across the country. I could easily hang up or block his ass. Now that he was there in the flesh, I wanted to rip his ass apart.

On top of all that, a nigga was backed up sexually. Shayne was home, but we weren't on that level with each other. She barely allowed me to touch her or hold her at night when she did get in bed. Shorty was traumatized, and I was at a loss on how to help her other than just being there.

Chapter 7
Wood

A couple of weeks later...

"Where you going?" Ledger was seated on the edge of the bed that Lis and I had been sharing.

Standing in the mirror, I adjusted the collar to my shirt and took him in. Nigga was like my little shadow these days. When I moved, he moved. He was always wanting to be under me and learn new shit. With a half-suppressed laugh, I shook my head and spun to face him.

"I gotta go to the club and deal with some business. Grand opening is this weekend. I want to get that out of the way, so I can be more active for Lishan and all her appointments coming up with the baby."

"She's been real quiet lately," Ledger noted, very observant.

"I know. She told you about the video, right?"

"Yeah." Humbled, he bowed his head as his eyes fell on the ground.

I had been irritable for who knows how long. Just when

things were getting on track with Lishan, we got hit with some more bullshit. The tape of her performing getting leaked pulled her back into a turtle shell. She barely wanted to leave the house. Security was so tight around our spot that they were checking in, even when they didn't need to. Wylde and I had already touched base, so if one of them was moving, we all knew about it. There was even a group text with just the four of us in it, letting the others know how we were moving day to day in our households.

Adjusting the thick ass Cuban link across my chest, I examined Ledger in the mirror, watching me. Lil nigga had become my little brother in a short amount of time. Him and Linc were both looking up to me like the big brother they never had. I did my best to be a good influence, but I was no saint. The youngster was wise beyond his years and knew how to hold shit down. Only thing I hadn't done was show him how to shoot yet, but fucking with me, he was gon' learn one way or another.

Lishan had been tight ever since Merlin leaked the video, but with my reassurance, she was able to push through. I was proud of her. At first, she sat in bed for about a week, letting that shit get the best of her. Between me and Shayne, she wouldn't succumb to the bullshit. Even with having to keep up with the kids, doctor's appointments, and her school schedule, shit was admirable. I bought her a new laptop and shit, so she didn't have to worry about going to the library or borrowing mine. She was grateful and told me it was too much, but she didn't know I wanted her to be happy and would do whatever I could to make that happen.

With the grand opening of the club coming up, shit was a little tense all around. I had been falling back from the real estate shit and letting Wylde handle it. That was always more his speed. He took over in LA when our father fell back from his duties. I always thought there was more to it. Right after my moms died, there was a shift within the family. Wylde and Waker had been on the fence for as long as I could remember. On one level, he was proud of bro and loved him wholeheartedly. Wylde was also the golden child. Everything he did came naturally to him. For me, I didn't care. The fame and all that other shit wasn't what I was worried about. I wanted the money above all else. I was also more confident in myself than a mothafucka gave me credit for.

My relationship with Wylde wasn't about competition either. He was four years older than me, so I knew he already knew the game and was just trying to teach it to me. There was no envy or jealousy where we were concerned, though. I was one of the few who knew Wylde didn't like all that attention anyway. I was the star in the family, and he was more than willing to let me have that.

All his life, he had been propped up. Everything he achieved seemed to be for someone else, whether it was our mother, our father, or even Rich. As much as those three banked on him, he never wanted to let them down. He might have gotten involved in the streets and running our gun ring, but it wasn't something that he desired or strived for. It just turned out to be another thing he was good at. Pops used to always drill in my head how shit came naturally to dudes like him and Rich. A lot of times, he seemed pretty resentful of his oldest son and his big brother. Shit was ridiculous, but it reminded me of the times I did hear him and moms having words. She was always telling him to let stuff go when he went on his rants, but he couldn't. He would get a few drinks in him, and it would turn into a session of him playing 'what if' on his life.

"How you feel about it?" I asked, dismissing my own problems and facing him.

"I think somebody needs to beat Merlin's ass and teach him

how to show other people respect. I hate him." Ledger glowered.

"Don't worry about that. You just a kid. Focus on school and making sure your little brother and sister are good. I'll take care of the grown folks shit," I assured him, patting his shoulder. "I'm gon' head out. You good?"

"I'm good. I was going to start prepping dinner and stuff." He rose from the bed, and we padded to the door together.

Misael and the little ones were posted up in the living room when I came down the stairs. Grabbing my letterman jacket off the coat rack, I pulled it on and hovered as they all seemed to focus on the movie playing.

"I'll be back later. Y'all be easy. Ledger, put me a plate up. Don't play with me, bro." I aimed a warning finger on my way out.

No lie, nigga could cook like somebody's old ass granny. Even if he was just experimenting, shit was never a miss. I never wanted to miss a meal around this mothafucka. I had plans for him, and he didn't even know it. I had already gotten with our family accountant, my cousin Rashad, and had him set up accounts for all three kids and Lishan and the baby. I wasn't playing. It was easier to put money into shit like that than to blow it on a shopping spree. I already had plenty of fly shit. My goal was to use the money I had invested to make more money and keep me afloat, so I could have all the other luxuries I wanted as well.

About thirty minutes later, I parked in my reserved spot in the club parking lot and shut off my whip. When I got out and let myself into the building, I smelled incense burning as I checked the scene. Everything appeared as it should. The high ceilings had bright lights dangling from them. There were platforms scattered for women to dance on, and even a few cages in the air for live entertainment. We had auditioned some girls to dance in them with body paint and glitter all over them, giving the place a cosmic vibe. The moon shaped bar had silver stools surrounding it, and the shelves were all lined up along a wall that was actually a mirror too. Nodding to myself, I was impressed with the new look. This shit was going to be fire.

"What's good, partner?" D's voice dragged me from observing the setting as he and Noemi came from the back of the bar together.

Shorty had been eye fucking me for a while, and D either didn't notice or was playing blind to the shit.

"What's up?" I dapped him up and lifted my chin in greeting to Noemi as her tongue swiped anxiously over her lips.

"Shit looks good, right?" D brought a blunt to his lips and sparked it with his torch lighter.

"Hell yeah. We gon' kill the club scene." I nodded.

"Fuck, yeah. I appreciate you taking a chance, bro. Yo' people coming through for the opening, right?"

"Hell yeah. We gon' be in this mothafucka lit this weekend. I'm going up to the office now to finish some paperwork and pay these vendors. Make sure everybody got they personnel paperwork in too. I want all that shit processed so we don't have no problems."

"Aight." D bobbed his head, and I spun on my heel to take my ass upstairs to my office.

I unlocked my door, pushed it open, and let myself into my office space. Shit looked a lot cooler than it did when I first got there. The fish tank in the corner automatically lit up the room when I entered, but I still hit the lights. Dropping my keys on the bookshelf near the door, I peeled my jacket off and went to take a seat behind my desk. I took my phone out of my pocket along with the pack of woods I had been walking around with and tossed them both on the glass top to the desk before I pulled my mesh gaming chair out to take a seat. I had been reading over and signing off on shit for at least forty-five minutes when my phone chimed, letting me know I had a call coming through. Seeing *Baby Girl* dance across the screen, I swiped to pick up, pressing the phone against my ear and falling back in my chair.

"What's up, shorty?" Playing with my chin, I listened to her sigh.

"Am I bothering you?"

"No. What's wrong?" I asked, noticing the drop in her tone.

"Nothing. I don't want to bother you."

"Lis, you called for a reason. Don't do that. You hungry? Need me to send you some GrubHub or something? What you want?" I asked, putting the phone on speaker and going to my apps.

"No." She snickered. "Well..."

I smiled, knowing I had gotten her to crack one on the other side of the phone.

"You know you hungry. Yo' ass always is. What you want? Mexican, Chinese, Thai?" I scrolled through the different places on the app.

"You feel like eating with me?"

"Shit, I'm still at the club, but I ain't ate since earlier. Swing through. I'll just order something here and have it waiting for you."

"I want Pho and eggrolls," she requested.

"I gotchu."

"Okay. On my way." Lishan hung up the phone with renewed energy from what I could tell. She spent a lot of time in her own head, so it was up to me to pull her out of that shit. I didn't want her all sad and shit her whole pregnancy. That shit was not cool, and I didn't want my baby coming out with that kind of energy either. I went back to work, stopping briefly to take a piss. I had left the bathroom door open when I did so and didn't hear anybody come in as I tossed my head back and allowed my pipe to drain. When I was done, my head dropped, and I caught something in my peripheral through the mirror right beside the sink.

"Well, I see some things don't change," Noemi flirted as I shook my dick and tucked him away.

Zipping my pants, I faced her while adjusting my button and belt to my jeans as I looked her over in the tight, revealing lace catsuit she rocked. I was a man at the beginning and end of every fucking day, so there was no denying that she was fine as fuck, but I wasn't sweating her like that. I washed my hands, and Noemi took that as her cue to slide up behind me and reach for my semi hard dick.

"You ever think about me, Wood?" she asked, stroking him as I shut the water off. I shook her off as I reached for a paper towel.

"Honestly? Nah." Shaking my head, I faced her, and her expression fell in disappointment. "We spent a lot of time apart, No. So, you been off my radar."

"Well, I've kept up with you on Instagram. Still the same old Wood. Low key." Her dainty hand rested against my chest while her dark oval shaped eyes struck mine. "I still remember everything." Just as she started to lower herself, I quickly snatched her up, and our bodies collided.

"The fuck you on?"

"Shit, I'm trying to be on you." She cocked a brow, making a bold attempt to pull me into her web.

"Nah, this ain't what we doing."

Fastening her wrists together between us, I nudged her back as the door to my office opened, and in strolled the one thing that caused my heart to skip. These days, Lishan was fluent in whatever she did. A nigga was in literal awe of her. As soon as she stepped in, wearing her distressed jeans, tank top, and cardigan over it as her little pudge poked through her top, I knew shit was about to escalate. The warmth in her eyes instantly became shadowed with rage. She was holding our food in one hand as her arm dropped to her side.

"What the fuck is this!" She belted.

My mind spiraled to another time. This moment just triggered an odd realization about my family dynamic. I had my own issues with my mama. I never felt slighted, even though I knew everyone doted on Wylde for being the perfect son. He could have that shit. One thing I knew about my brother was, he never treated me different, and he was fair. We could be on opposite ends of the spectrum of some shit, but it didn't matter. Wylde never made me feel like I was stupid or slow. He listened to my ideas and always encouraged me if it was some shit he wanted to do. Waker rode him so much that it was his life's goal to exceed everything the old man did and make him eat his words to him over the years.

Waker was always hard on Wylde for one thing or another, even when he excelled at everything. For him, it was never good enough. His drinking habit along with the gambling didn't help. A lot of shit was swept under the rug over the years as far as the family was concerned. I always knew there were skeletons that everyone kept tucked away. I just never thought the shit existed in my own family. I knew my mama took plenty to the grave. She might have let Waker get away with the cheating and shit, but that man knew better than to ever disrespect her. I wasn't sure what kind of hold she had over him, but it was enough to get him to back down any time he thought he was going to challenge her. I didn't want a woman who would endure suffering for me or from me.

"Don't I know you?" Noemi squinted, her full glossy lips curving into a complacent smirk as she pulled me from my random thoughts.

"Noemi, get out. I don't know why you even came in here on this bullshit."

"The bitch must want her ass whupped." Lishan tossed the bag of food on my desk, and Noemi snickered.

"You're cute, little girl." Her eyes stretched, and she snapped her fingers. "Wait, now I know where I saw you. Oh, shit, you viral girl. Hmm, I guess somebody taught you well. You looked like a pro instead of this little ass girl standing in front of me right now." She sized her up.

I could read the fiery behind shorty's glare as she lunged for her, so I dove between them, keeping my back to my ex. Placing a hand on Lishan's growing stomach, I nudged her with some force, and she shot daggers into my eyes.

"Fall back. You ain't about to do shit with my baby in there."

"Baby?" Noemi repeated, her lip curling in distaste.

"That's what he said, bitch!"

"Shorty, I need you to calm the fuck down, aight."

"Wood, who the fuck is this bitch?" Lishan snapped, aiming her long nail over my shoulder.

"Oh, I'm the one responsible for that dick game, sweetie. You're welcome!"

"Wood—"

"I told you once already, Noemi. Get the fuck out," I growled over my shoulder.

"Show some damn respect, Wood. This is my man's club too. Remember that. You are his partner. He asked you to be a part of this. Y'all have a good evening. Maybe on some nights when we have performances, your girl here can provide the entertainment," she joked as she brushed past us.

The only thing keeping Lishan from going after her was the tight grip I forced on her wrist, keeping her right where she was. I went to close the door and lock it before spinning and soaking in her irate expression.

"Who the fuck is that bitch?"

"That's Noemi. We used to fuck around," I confessed.

"And now she's fucking the nigga who you are in business with?" Lishan's brows rose as her lips parted in disbelief. "Really, Wood?"

"What? That ain't got shit to do with me. I ain't fucking her no more." Shrugging, I marched over to the desk and started to dig the containers out of the bag.

"Why you didn't tell me then? You been working here for weeks with her."

"You got enough shit going on. I ain't trying to have you spazzing on me." I opened the lids and started to separate our meals on the desk.

Pulling out a chair, I put a hand to Lishan's hip and guided her over so she could sit down, and we could eat.

"I don't be spazzing." She rolled her eyes.

"But you be giving attitude and trying to withhold the pussy, and I ain't got time for that." I handed her the Pho bowl and a fork before digging an eggroll from the bag and taking a big bite. She snatched the plasticware from my hand and lifted the lid to her bowl.

"I don't like that bitch," she muttered, scooping some noodles onto her fork and turning her nose up.

"Shit, I didn't expect you to." I leaned against the desk and continued to eat while eyeing her thick legs in the pants she wore. "You ain't got shit to worry about, though. That's the last thing on my mind. I'm here to run a business. That's a complication I don't fucking need."

"Better not be." She pouted, eyes fixed on her bowl as she stirred it.

"What's wrong?"

"Nothing. I have a doctor's appointment tomorrow at noon, though. You think you can make this one?" she asked, lifting her eyes.

"Yeah. I can clear my morning. Is that it?"

"I don't know. I can't stop thinking about this whole situation with my daddy and Misael. Shit is just nagging me for some reason. I'm having a baby. I guess it just puts things in perspective. Thinking about grandparents, aunts, uncles, and all that. I can't exactly stay mad at Misael. He's dying already. I just feel like he should have kept it a buck with me. I've done nothing but take care of him and those kids. He owed me that much."

"I can't argue with you there, shorty. Maybe he thought he was doing the right thing."

"Maybe. It still wasn't his choice to make. Then, there's my mama. I'm so pissed off at her. That don't even sound right. She's dead. I don't know."

We ate and talked for a few before I walked her outside to my extra car that I had her driving until the whip I chose for her came through. Once she was in the driver's seat of the Jeep, I planted a soft kiss to her lips, which made her smile when we parted.

"I'm going to grab a few things from the store, so I can make dinner tomorrow. The kids want my alfredo lasagna. Ledger also has basketball tryouts at 3:30 p.m." She tossed her purse into the passenger seat.

"Okay. Text me when you get to the house. I'll be in a little late, but I'll let you know when I'm on the way." Once she was in the car, I patted the hood and watched her back out of her spot and pull off.

Spinning toward the door, I caught Noemi coming out with a fresh cigarette in her hand, blowing smoke as she wrapped her leather jacket tighter around herself.

"Since when you a cradle robber? I always thought you preferred your women a little more seasoned."

"You mad salty, Noemi. Why? You got a nigga, so what you worried about me and my baby mama for?"

"Please," she scoffed, taking another pull from the cigarette. "Everybody done seen yo' baby mama's goods. Aint nothing special there. If a nigga wants to see what yo' woman working with, all he gotta do is pull that shit up on the internet. The least she could do was get paid like Only Fans."

I inched into Noemi's space, causing her breath to pause in her chest as I backed her into the wall of the building. Bringing a hand against her chest, I squeezed her throat and searched her eyes with menace bouncing around mine.

"Who the fuck are you to judge anybody? You got more bodies than a fucking cemetery, No. Let's not forget you been ran through, shorty. What makes you better than the next? Lishan made a mistake and trusted a fuck nigga who was helping her get money. What was your excuse? She might be taking her clothes off to get paid, but at least she ain't on her back every day and calling that shit a career. Does D know about your past?" I queried, noticing her eyes light up at the notion. "Nah, I imagine he don't. I can't see how, when you been doing the shit since you was a teenager. I forgot, there's power in the pussy, and most of these niggas can still fuck if they want to for a fee. Am I right?"

"Fuck you, Wood! If you only knew, nigga!" she spat, dropping her cigarette.

"Nah, been there. Done that." Releasing her neck, I stepped away from her with a smile. "Stay the fuck away from Lishan. Don't even speak to her when you see her, or me for that matter." I yanked the door open and stepped back inside, leaving her shook outside as she caught her breath.

Shayne

A couple of nights later...

"Uncle Wood, you said you would be here at seven o'clock." Storm padded into the foyer with her iPhone held up and facing her.

"Storm, you gon' quit thinking you run me, lil mama. I'm what they call fashionably late." I could hear Wood's voice as I descended the stairs, holding my silver Stuart Weitzman clutch close as I took my time in matching three-inch heels.

Stopping in the mirror in the hallway just next to the door, I adjusted my dress on my shoulders and turned to the side while sucking in my stomach. I wasn't that far along to be showing, but after two kids already, pregnancy hit different, and I could tell from the cup size I had gone up in my bra as well as my dress that I was damn sure with child. I did my best to contain it. I wasn't sure how long I would be able to sweep it under the rug like it wasn't happening. I managed to sneak off to a doctor's appointment, telling everyone that I had a nail appointment and swearing the guard to silence when I changed the route to the salon.

So far everything was good with the baby. I started taking prenatal vitamins, which made me sick. I told the doctor the only thing that kept me going was cannabis, and she agreed that as long as it was in small doses, it was fine, but she also recommended a prescription for some anti-nausea medicine. She dismissed me with a clean bill of health after running a complete screening on me for STDs and told me to follow up in one month.

"Ooh, Mommy, you look so pretty," Storm gushed, peeling her eyes away from her conversation enough to widen her eyes and smile.

"You think so?"

"Uncle Wood, don't she look good?" She spun the phone, and I could see Wood seated in the limo.

They were more than likely on their way to the house to pick us up. Tonight was the grand opening of Prized Package, and it was up! Although I couldn't drink, a little THC or CBD put me at ease during these times and kept me from getting as sick. The stench of alcohol turned my stomach anyway.

"She look aight." Wood gave an eyeroll, and Lishan popped into the camera beside him.

"Lemme see." She nudged him and took the phone. "Oh shit, titties! Girl put them things away! You look gorgeous though, sis. We're on the way."

"Well, I don't know where Wylde is, so—"

"He's in the office, Mommy. He said he had some work to do before he left." Storm turned the phone back to herself. "Tell Lumi we having a sleepover in my room, girls only."

"Bye, Storm. We'll be there in a few, Shayne." The call ended, and I did one last take of myself in the mirror.

The canary yellow off the shoulder dress had a slit up one thigh and was blinged the hell out, giving it a very shimmery look as it swayed when I walked. With Cartier dangling from my wrists, neck, and ears, I let go of another breath as I heard a door open and close nearby. Wylde was closing the door to the office he had taken over, sharp in a black suit with a tie and matching pocket square the same color as my dress.

"Damn," I muttered, loins tingling as I soaked him in all fine and shit.

We had been in proximity for a little over a week now, and things had been tense. In the bedroom, things were lacking. Either he was up all night, or I was. It was getting better the further along I got in this pregnancy. The cannabis was also easing my nerves and making it easier for me to sleep. Things were still more distant than I cared for, though. Seeing him in that moment took me back to the first night we were together after the fundraiser. Something about us in our formal wear ignited sparks.

"Mmm." He bit his bottom lip as he approached, resting one hand on my hip and pulling me to him. "This shit fire right here, mama." He greeted me with a kiss.

"And you are fine in this damn suit." I played with the collar and stood on my toes to place another peck to his lips. "We clean up nice."

"Yeah. Should be a good night. I'm proud of Wood."

"I can't believe he's going to be a daddy." The words hit me a little harder than intended as it dawned on me that Wylde was too, and he had no idea.

My hand fell from his shoulder, and I cleared my throat as I stepped away from him.

"What's wrong?" he asked, concern flitting across his face.

"Nothing."

"Something is up witchu." He wouldn't allow me to pull away as he dragged me back into his space.

"Wylde, tonight is about Wood and his success. I just want to be present. These last few weeks have been hell. I want to go out and enjoy the night with the people I care about. I know you're leery about me going back to work, but you are always the one telling me not to live in fear. So much has already been taken from me, from us."

"You right." Wylde nodded as the doorbell rang.

Cuffing some of my ass, he cupped my chin and tongued me down again with passion. Immediately, my mound responded.

"Wait! Let me take a picture. You look like a prince and princess." Storm held her device up and snapped a shot of us hugged up together.

I went to answer the door when we were done, and Wylde

scooped her into his arms so he could take a peek at the photo with her. When I flung the door open, Wood and Lishan were arguing on the other side but immediately turned into all smiles when they saw me and came barreling past. Lumi and Linc took off like a blur ahead of them.

"What are y'all arguing about?" I asked.

"Girl, I took this fool to my first doctor's appointment, and let's just say, he is not required to go to any beyond this point," Lishan joked and shook her head.

"All I asked was can the baby feel the dick when I'm inside her? I just want to make sure I ain't fucking my son's head up while I'm in pound town."

"It could be a girl," Lishan pointed out.

"Oh my God, there are children present." I peered around as Wylde lowered Storm to the ground, and Nael appeared with San at his side from the kitchen.

"That's why I said pound town, sis."

"And dick!" I hissed.

"Why you got to be repeating shit? It's kids around," Wood jested, causing me to swing on him as he chuckled. "Nah, but you look good, though. Y'all all coordinated and shit." He looked us over.

Lishan was in a mauve colored sequined dress with a diagonal sheer piece across her chest, and a slit decorated in lighter colored feathers up her left thigh. Like Wylde, Wood's tie and pocket square were the same color as her dress, and they were both red carpet ready. Lishan had her locs styled in a pin-up style and her face was perfectly beat in a smokey eyed look with eye shadow to match her dress.

"Pictures! Pictures!" Storm squealed.

We stood and snapped a few together before Wood checked the time on his iced out Presidential.

"Aight, we gotta go. Fashionably late was about twenty minutes ago."

"This shit start when we get there. Fuck that." Wylde adjusted his blazer once again as I held my clutch close.

"Okay." I faced the kids and held my arms open. "Hugs." I embraced San and Storm first, but Lumi and Linc quickly stepped forward too.

We had all been spending time back and forth between houses lately, so we had formed our own little family, and I was something like their auntie. Lishan had done right by them, and they were all well behaved and so sweet. Lumi was a little firecracker, but I loved how close she and Storm had gotten in such a short amount of time.

"Y'all be good. Don't give Nael hell," Lishan warned after they all surrounded her too.

"Have fun and be safe." Nael walked us all to the door.

Lishan was determined to turn up, pregnant and all, so we cranked the *Renaissance* album by Beyonce the whole way, pissing Wood and Wylde off as we sang along word for word and popped our shit. By the time we got to the club, all eyes were on us as we piled out of the limo and walked the red carpet together. They were a couple of news outlets and podcasts on the scene with their microphones trying to get a sound bite from Wood as he clutched Lishan close, and she beamed with all thirty-two teeth on his arm. He was so calm and smooth, along with Wylde as he hugged me from behind, and we posed for a picture together.

The smile on my face dwindled when I saw that his father had arrived. What caused my face to light up was the sight of Rich at his side. I pulled away from Wylde and rushed to hug him.

"Rich!"

"Well, it's good to see you too, Shayne." He held me and laughed.

"I didn't know you were coming." Pulling back, I checked him out in the black and charcoal gray suit he wore.

Beside him, Waker observed me with disdain. It was obvious that this man didn't like me. It was strange, since I didn't know him, but it didn't matter to me because I wasn't familiar with him either.

"Wood extended an invitation a few weeks ago, and I told him I would do everything I could to get here," Rich explained.

"How long are you here?" I asked, intertwining my hand with his as we approached Wylde together.

"A couple of weeks. Things in London are stabilizing. I have a great staff, so I can afford a little time off." Rich and Wylde dapped each other up and shook hands.

"Yo, let's make it inside! We gotta make an entrance!" Wood threw an arm across Lishan's shoulders, and we all trailed them inside.

There was a slight pause with the DJ when Wood appeared. A big announcement was made like this fool was a local celebrity. Bitches were drooling, and niggas were green with envy, but everyone greeted him with applause and loud cheers. Taking a peek up at Wylde, I could see the pride all over him as he allowed Wood to soak in his moment. It was a sight.

The music turned back up, lights flickered, and smoke floated through the air like clouds. It was something to see the girls on the platforms and inside the cages dancing erotically to the beat. Bottles were popped all over, and the bottle girls were scantily dressed while carrying them along with sparklers through the club.

The entire space was rocking. Sweat, with all the different scents of cologne and perfume floated around along with the smoke and alcohol stench. I could tell that folks were already having a good time. Ladies were free before ten, so of course we outnumbered the men. There was some paparazzi inside as well. Wylde pulled me extra close as we squeezed through the crowd. Wood made sure to set us up with a sky view over the entire club. Nobody was touching us in our section.

As the bass kicked in, Wylde coolly swayed behind me. He didn't dance, but he could hold a beat and sway with me. He was alert more than anything. Him and Wood were on ten. They blew a blunt on the ride over but barely took a sip of their champagne.

Once we got to our private room, I noticed that it was surrounded by glass so thick that you would need a laser to cut through it. I leaned toward Lishan as she grabbed a bottle of champagne.

"I may not be able to drink, but you can." She reached for an empty flute and popped the cork.

I took the glass, but I had no plans to drink the shit. She would be lucky if I made a fake attempt to swallow it before dumping it. Leaning closer, I lowered my voice as she busily moved about. She was in full hostess mode, which was odd since this wasn't her event. She wanted to be in full support of Wood, though. I knew it left her on edge that he was the owner of a club though. A lot of bullshit went on in clubs, and she didn't want Wood to get caught up in it.

"How is Wood to you?" I asked, leaning in.

I didn't have to lower my voice because it was loud, and they were too busy greeting everyone who had come out to support and getting in their zone.

"I don't know. He's Wood." Lishan shrugged. "You know that nigga gon' be him in whatever environment. Why? What's wrong?" Immediately, she went taut as her hands fell on her hips, and she carefully skimmed me.

"I'm just asking. Shit has been too quiet."

"Shayne, you are always looking for the BS. That's what's wrong with you," she accused, grabbing a plate and stacking a few wings, all flats, on it.

"Oh, so you analyzing me too now?"

"All I am saying is, you need to relax," she emphasized. "I can't deal with you constantly peeking around the corner for the next bad thing."

"That's because the next bad thing is always out there lurking, Lishan." She handed me a plate, and I started to stack it with finger food.

"Have something to eat. I plan on you drinking enough for us both." She brushed me off.

I grabbed a drum and took a bite while cutting my eyes across the room as Waker waltzed in with none other than Kaori's pinhead ass.

I swear I couldn't stand that bitch. She irked every single bad nerve in my body.

"So, since I'm always looking for the next bad thing, tell me, Lis, the fuck this bitch been doing around Wylde?"

She tensed up beside me, so I instantly knew it was going to be some shit I didn't want to hear.

"Why does it matter? He put her in her place and made it clear that you are his priority. That's that shit I'm talking about."

"So, if you disappeared for over a month, and Wood was around some other bitch, you would be okay with it?" She wasn't prepared for my line of questioning as she sucked the sauce from the meatballs that she had plated for herself off her thumb and reached for a plastic fork.

"See, what you not about to do is come for me!"

"What y'all over here talking about?" Wood popped up

with Wylde at his side as Lishan and I cut our eyes at each other.

Neither of us were ready to spill this conversation. She grabbed some fresh broccoli off her plate and dipped it in ranch while I took a gulp of the champagne, which I knew damn well I shouldn't have been drinking.

"Nothing." I tipped the glass to my lips anyway and instantly regretted it once I swallowed. I was fucking up, and immediately I knew it was going to come back up at some point.

"Damn, give us a minute to all toast together, sis," Wood derided.

"I umm, I need to use the bathroom." The bubbles wouldn't even travel into my digestive system.

I could feel them tickling my throat as I located the nearest bathroom and rushed inside. There were at least five stalls. All appeared to be empty except the one on the very end, and I didn't give a fuck who heard me. Falling over the toilet in the first stall, I spilled the contents in my stomach as the main door swung open.

"Shayne, what the hell is wrong with you?" Lishan's voice bounced off the small space. "And don't say nothing. Something has been off with you since you got back. You won't talk about it, but we all know."

Once I was satisfied that nothing else was coming out of me, I sat up, flushed the toilet, and stumbled out of the stall. She stood tall in the mirror as she fixed her hair and applied a coat of gloss to her lips before puckering them. I reached to wash my hands.

Lishan pinched her lips together as her face balled up in disgust.

"Okay, which one of us is pregnant here again?"

When my eyes met hers in the mirror while I washed my

mouth out with warm water, hers nearly doubled as she fell against the sink and held onto it for support.

"Oh, shit!"

"Lishan," I groaned, lowering my head before reaching for a paper towel from the holder.

"Are you fucking pregnant?" she whispered in excitement.

"I can't do this with you." Gripping the sink, my head sank as I took in a few breaths.

"Oh, really? Who else you going to do it with? Does Wylde even know?"

"No, he doesn't, and I'm not ready to tell him." I patted my face and neck dry before tossing the paper towel into the trash can.

"Here, have one of these." She held out a Ziploc bag with a couple of Hawaiian rolls tucked inside. "It will stabilize you. You can't go back out there looking like that. He's going to know. Wood can always tell when I don't feel good. I don't know how that nigga knows me so well already."

"You just walking around with food in your bag?" I grabbed a roll and took a bite.

It was surprisingly good, and I was almost hallway done when I decided I needed an outlet. Tonight just had to be the night for the shit.

"Girl, Merlin's mama got me on that shit. I spent a lot of time in clubs and was a lightweight with alcohol, but it was all I could do to have the nerve to dance. So, she wanted to make sure I never got sloppy, so her ass kept some bread, crackers, and whatever around for me to eat. Anyway... why haven't you told him?"

"The same reason we haven't talked about everything else." I breathed heavily. "Wylde blew into my life like this breath of fresh air. He just had this urgency to step forward and be there for me and the kids. He stole my heart damn near day one. I didn't expect it. Then I saw him with San and Storm. He was so strong and dependable. He was everything they needed."

"He was everything that *you* needed," Lishan corrected.

"Maybe. Elim got in the way of that. I mean, it's been a week, and he hasn't touched me other than a few kisses. Something is between us, and..."

"Maybe it's you," Lishan pointed out.

"Nah, that ain't it," I argued, shaking my head.

"Shayne, is this Wylde's baby?"

"Yes," I quickly answered.

"Then what is the problem? Talk to him."

"Is he going to believe me? I was with Elim for weeks, Lishan. I might have been high out of my mind most of that time due to him and his mama constantly force feeding me narcotics, but... I knew what was going on. I was his toy. He enjoyed taking advantage of me. It gave him some kind of sick thrill. How do I tell Wylde I'm pregnant and some shit like that?"

"First, stop being so dramatic. You need to relax. Do you realize that we are going to be pregnant together?" Her eyes sparkled as she grabbed both of my wrists.

"I don't know what I'm going to do."

"Pssh, girl, it will all figure itself out." She waved me off.

The toilet flushed in the last stall before the door opened. When Kaori stepped out, I damn near shit a brick. Had I known this bitch was present, I damn sure wouldn't have spilled my guts. Her face had almost healed from me beating her ass, and she used makeup to cover the rest. She was just as superior as she was that day, and it instantly gave me flashbacks as my fist balled on its own.

"Well, you seem to have made a nice recovery," Lishan teased, pouting her lips in the mirror after applying a coat of gloss.

Kaori stopped at the sink to wash her hands. "Yeah, and you hear all kinds of things in public places." Her gaze fell on me. "I wonder how Wylde will feel when he finds out what you've been hiding."

My chest swelled in fear, and Lishan and I eyed each another. This bitch was cruising for another ass whupping. I was blocking the door, but she didn't seem shaken in the least.

"That ain't your business to tell."

"Well, he deserves to know that you're keeping things from him. Wylde is big on trust. I know him better than you. In fact, we got reacquainted very well while you were away. I spent a lot of time in his bed, and he spent a lot of time inside me. He didn't seem too lonely or lost without you during those times either."

Lishan caught the fury in my eyes and stepped between us.

"Shayne, let's go." Grabbing my shoulders, she forced me to spin toward the door and she was right behind me.

"Lishan—" I whipped around on her once we were in the hallway.

"Let it go. She ain't even worth it. You already beat her ass once."

Kaori strut out confidently, a smirk dancing across her lips as she brushed past us. I almost lunged for her again as she strolled off with her head held high.

Lishan and I trailed her through the club until she arrived in our section with all the men. Standing around with flutes that they sipped from when we approached, I noticed that there seemed to be some tension in the air.

"Everything good?" Wylde queried, tilting his glass to his lips.

His gaze darted from me to Kaori.

"Oh, yes, everything is good. I was in the bathroom with

your girl here. You learn all kinds of things when you end up in the right place at the right time."

"The fuck is she talking about?" Still holding his flute, he aimed a finger at Kaori, but his focus was on me.

"I need to talk to you," I muttered.

"Why don't I share the news for you?" Kaori piped up.

"Why don't you mind your own fucking business!" I screeched and watched her face tighten up before she snickered.

"You made it my business when you turned the bathroom into your confessional," Kaori declared. "Why don't you ask her what she's been up to when she wasn't with you? Ask her about her ex and the things they did together. You want to play hero to a bitch who was fucking her ex after she left you on stuck. That's not even the best part, though."

Wylde slowly swallowed the rest of his drink before he set his glass on a table.

"Shut up!" I got in her face, sending her cowering back as she lingered at Wylde's father's side.

"Shayne, the fuck is she talking about?"

"Wylde, can we go somewhere and talk, please?" Tears piled into my eyes, causing them to sting as my heart fell into my stomach.

"My office." Wood slid him a key, which Wylde accepted as he pushed me through the club.

It was slowly growing more packed as his large hand landed on my back. He used the key to let us into Wood's office and closed the door behind us. The fish tank illuminated the room, but Wylde hit the light switch anyway. Wringing my hands together, I paced as he tucked both of his muscular arms over his squared chest.

"What's this about, Shayne? The fuck is Kaori talking about?"

"I told you what was happening to me. How I was being drugged into submission. What did you think he did to me during those times, Wylde? I couldn't control it or stop it."

"So, you were fucking him?"

"Yes," I answered shamefully as my head lowered.

Swiping his hand down his face, he bobbed his head. "What else you been hiding?" he demanded.

"I'm pregnant," I blurted out.

A sudden weight lifted from my shoulders when I let that truth off my chest.

"You... preg... how long have you known this?" He could barely finish a sentence as his dark eyes raked over me.

"Since you brought me to the safehouse. Screw told me when I woke up."

"He didn't say shit to me," he mumbled.

"He wasn't sure I even knew, so he kept it to himself and waited for me to wake up."

"You couldn't tell me that? You been back for over a week!" The sudden rise in his octave caused me to flinch as a tear slipped past my cheek.

"Because I didn't want to have this conversation!"

"So, you'd rather avoid it? How the fuck is that working for you, Shayne? You didn't think I deserved to know you walking around here pregnant by this mothafucka—"

"The baby is yours," I clarified, sniffling and wiping away the tear that fell. Disbelief fell over his face. "Screw said I was seven weeks. I was only with Elim for five."

Wylde remained shocked in front of me, looking me over carefully as he pressed his back against the office door.

"We can do a DNA test if you want. I already saw my doctor. She said the baby is doing fine, and they ran tests to make sure I was okay physically as well. She signed off on a clean bill of health. I was going to tell you when I could process it all myself. So much has been happening, and I've been fighting like hell just to stay sober enough to make it through the day. You don't understand how hard it is trying to block all the things he did to me from my mind."

"I told you to talk to someone, even if it's not me."

"You think I want to relive that shit?" My brows came together as he straightened up on his feet.

"What else are you going to do? Keep brushing the shit off like it didn't happen? Is that helping you? You been going around here lying to everybody—"

"I wasn't lying."

"You damn sure wasn't telling the truth!" he barked in my face.

He swept a hand over the top of his head before moving it back and forth.

"Wylde—"

"I'm not about to do this right now. This is Wood's night, and I ain't trying to fuck this up for him. I'm going to get a drink." His hand landed on the doorknob, and I reached for his shoulder.

He stiffened under my touch, and I pulled back.

"Please—"

"Shayne, leave me alone right now," he warned, flinging the door open and rushing into the hall as the bass from the club vibrated the walls.

I remained behind as I choked on tears. Closing the door, I pressed my forehead against it and endured the weeping as it washed over me. *God, how did I let this happen?* He was never going to forgive me. Spinning around, I rested my back on the door and slowly eased into a sitting position on the floor. This was not how I wanted to deliver this news to him. We were supposed to talk, and I would tell him everything, and we would decide together how to move forward. Now, he was doubting me and everything I told him. Burying my face in my hands, I let the tears fall as someone tapped lightly on the door.

"Shayne, its me," Lishan said from the other side.

"I just need a minute," I muttered.

"Okay. If you want to go, we can. That bitch Noemi just came to our section with her man." I could hear the annoyance in her tone.

She had told me about Wood's ex, but I had never met her. Bringing myself to my feet, I pulled the door open, and she strolled inside. I went to use the bathroom to clean my face up.

"You okay?" Lishan asked once I opened the door.

I stood at the sink washing my hands as she hovered behind me. Peering up in the mirror, I caught her staring at me.

"How did he take it?"

"Well, he doesn't want to talk to me or look at me." I sighed. "I should go. You stay. This is Wood's night. He wants you here. I'm not going to be any good to anybody."

"You can't change what happened. Wylde will be fine."

"I don't know, Lis. He was so upset."

"You are carrying his baby. He will get over it. Give it some time. Let's go grab some food and dance. I guess you shouldn't be drinking either, so we can at least pig out together." She slung an arm across my shoulders and reeled me toward her.

I was so grateful for her, especially since being back. I had never been one who was big on female friendships to begin with, but Lishan was that girl. She could hype me up, talk me down, and give me the harsh truth, even if I didn't want it. She was a blessing.

Chapter 8
Wylde

Instead of going to join everyone else, I went to the fucking bar. Shayne had fucked my head up, and a nigga needed something stronger than champagne. I ordered a double tequila and tossed it back with little effort before I signaled for the bartender to bring me another one. A strong hand rested on my shoulder, and when I peered up, I caught Rich staring down at me. His brow flicked up as he grabbed the empty seat beside where I stood.

"This is a nice setup. I like this look for Wood." He nodded as he took in the high ceilings that had flickering lights bouncing off the silver motif that hung from them.

"Yeah," I agreed, taking another sip from my glass and nodding.

"What's going on with you?"

"Not sure. I just learned for the second time this year that I was going to be a father. This time, it's with a woman who came in and stole my heart, ripped that shit up, and somehow managed to put it back in my chest and make it beat harder for her. Only her." I peered into my glass and shook my head.

"Hmm, that sounds familiar," Rich conveyed, clenching his hands together in front of him as his gaze veered ahead.

He ordered a whiskey and turned to me.

"Came in and knocked you off your fucking square. You didn't expect it, couldn't prepare for it, and now you're in the thick of it," Rich translated.

He had broken that down in a nutshell as I swallowed the rest of my drink.

"You sound like you know something about that."

Now that I thought about it, I had never known him to have a woman. He always entertained them, but as far as getting married or having a relationship, Rich remained on some solo shit. He didn't have any children or anything. He didn't really have attachments, which I had also noticed. I looked up to him because I always thought he was cool and fly, but sometimes it did seem like he was lonely.

"There was a woman, a long time ago." Rich brought his glass to his lips.

"What happened to her?"

"She chose another man," Rich responded. "I had to eat that. It wasn't all on her. My actions caused her to do so."

"So, that was it?" I pried.

Never knowing this about him left my interest piqued. It was obvious from his downcast eyes and the way he was trying to hold back the emotion in his voice that this was still something that cut him 'til this day.

"It had to be. We went our separate ways."

"But you never married anybody or kept a woman, Rich," I pointed out.

"No, I didn't. Like you said. Only her." He gulped the rest of his drink before glancing my way with a melancholy glint. "It didn't matter if I was with someone else, because when I was done with them, that was it. There were a few women over the years that I kept around more than once. The world is full of beautiful women, after all. I don't know. You just don't get that fulfillment that you do with that one. Trust me."

That was something I could relate to. Shayne came into my life when I was at a reflective point. She intrigued me. There was something very soft but fierce about her. Her beauty knocked me off my fucking feet. Her smooth brown skin, those big brown eyes that drank me in with appreciation, and those full lips that I wanted to kiss every time I was near her. She was an endorphin all day. When I was around her, it was just organic. Lately, I didn't know what the hell it was, but we seemed to be skipping chapters on each other or reading ahead. Either way, we weren't on the same fucking page, and her not telling me some shit of this proportion was proof of that.

"Yeah." I half turned, noticing Shayne coming down the steps with Lishan.

From across the room, she sensed me staring at her. She said something to Lishan and then turned to go in the other direction. It was obvious she was trying to leave, and Lishan was begging her to stay. Shayne shook her head, gave her a hug, and walked toward the back exit. Where the fuck did she think she was going without saying anything?

"I'll be back." I rushed off behind Shayne just as she reached the doors with the exit sign above them.

"Where the fuck you think you going, Shayne?"

"Why do you care?" she shouted over her shoulder.

"Hold up, aight." Taking a breath, I came up behind her just as her hands touched the crash bar on the door.

She dropped her head, and I noticed her shoulders shake. I knew she was fucking crying. Swiping my beard, I did my best to calm myself because my own chest felt like it was about to cave. The power this woman had over me was so deep-seated that I carried it with me even when I tried to shake that shit.

Draping an arm around her midsection, I pulled her against me, and she fell apart in my arms.

"I'm toxic, Wylde. Don't you see that? Everything in my life might as well be put at risk, and it's all because of me. My family is gone. My daddy is never waking up. I hold onto that because it makes me feel better. I know he's not coming back. I almost lost my kids. I put a target on all of us."

"You didn't do anything but fall for a manipulative, controlling, narcissistic bitch nigga. A nigga that never deserved you to begin with. You got two beautiful kids out of that, though, and they saved you. They are the reason you are the woman you are. You put them first. I've seen it. You sacrifice for them, and you take shit so that they don't have to. That's what I know about you. That's what I love about you." My words caused her to face me.

Some of her mascara ran as tears stained her cheeks and she blinked back more.

"You got a good heart, mama. It gets you fucked up sometimes, but that's because you a real one, and a lot of mothafuckas don't know how to deal with that because they all used to faking."

"You said you love something about me." A smile toyed with the corners of her mouth.

"I love everything about you because a nigga in love with you," I admitted.

"I love you too," she whispered, stepping into my space and wrapping her arms around my waist.

Holding her back, I cupped some of her chin with my free hand and planted a kiss that was just supposed to console her. She deepened it with her tongue, and her arms tightened around me as I squeezed a handful of her plump bottom. I didn't know how I hadn't picked up on that pregnancy shit with how she was filling out. When I met her, she was petite and had curves, but she was starting to spread in the hips and ass region since she'd been back.

"So, we going back in here to turn up or what?"

"You can turn up. I'll eat and dance, though."

"Bet. Come one." Grabbing her hand, I led her back to our section.

When I took my seat in one of the powder blue booths, I grabbed her and propped her across my lap. Kaori was in our section too, seated with my pops, who was on some chill shit but still mugging me every now and again. When he arrived, I didn't have shit to say. I still didn't. Him and K were both lucky they weren't escorted the fuck up out of there. I really wasn't trying to show my ass, but both of them were taking me there.

"Aye, Pop, you want that bitch to be a part of the family so bad, why don't you fuck with her?" I suggested, bringing my glass to my lips.

"Shit," Wood hissed, cautiously peering at Waker as he sat forward with a dark shadow building in his stare.

"The fuck you just say?"

"I mean, you fucked her mama, right? She's always around, and you spending all this time with her, making sure she good."

"Wylde, you know it's not even like that." Kaori tried to give her two cents.

"Maybe it should be. Maybe it will keep both of you the fuck out of my life." I guzzled the rest of my drink, and Wood leaned toward me.

"Was that really necessary?"

"Fuck them." I scoffed as someone turned the music up.

For the next hour or so, we partied, had drinks, and ate enough to keep us all full for the night. Lishan and Shayne danced until they were out of breath and their feet ached. Wood and I sat back chopping it up with a couple of the people from the office, and my brother did his thing as he moved through the crowd, getting to know people.

Taking a glance at my watch, I saw that it was pushing 2:00 am. I was lit, but I was still on point and observing. Kaori had eyes on me and Shayne most of the night, but we weren't paying her no mind. As far as I was concerned, her and my father could both take their asses back to LA. I wasn't there for the bullshit. Shayne and I had enough problems, and I didn't want either of them to be another interference.

When the girls went to dance, I sat back with Wood, blowing a blunt as the women remaining in our section danced all over each other. We entertained ourselves and watched right along with the other men in the vicinity. Kaori was hawking a nigga now that I was alone, and the shit was irritating as hell. I hated a bitch who didn't know how to let some shit go or when to move the fuck around.

"How long you gon' hold the past against Pop?" Wood's query interrupted my thoughts.

"Until he holds himself accountable and stops trying to force shit on me," I answered, pulling from the blunt and keeping the smoke in my lungs. "I don't owe him shit."

"Maybe not, but he is still our father."

"In name only. Why is he even here? Why is he forcing this shit with K? You ain't ask yourself that? The nigga don't do shit for nothing. There is always a motive behind it."

"Maybe he thought he was doing something for you. I mean we all thought you and K would end up together over the years. From Ma, to her mama, and even him."

"I made that shit clear when I chose Billie that it wasn't happening."

"And now Billie ain't in the picture," Wood pointed out. "You can see where he might think otherwise. You ain't gotta tell me what it is. I know the shit with Shayne is legit."

"She's pregnant," I revealed, surprising Wood.

"No shit?"

"Yeah, and she's been fucked up after all this shit with Elim and the kids. The things that nigga did to her..." I shook my head. "I know I can't protect her from everything, but it just pissed me off and reminded me of the kind of man I am, and the kind that he is." I bobbed my head across the way to where Waker sat.

"He's a fucking coward, bro. I don't ever want to be compared to him again. All my life, I looked up to him, even when he was talking down or riding me all the time. All I ever wanted to do was make him proud, and it seemed like no matter what I did, I fell short. I'm done with that. I stand on the fact that I am a better man. Say what you want."

"Nah, you got every right to that. I think the last couple of months has changed all of us in one way or another," Wood surmised.

Rich stood, and not too much later, Waker got up right after him. I found the shit odd, but sipped my drink and didn't think much else of it as Wood got up to handle something across the room with the bar. Kaori slid into the empty space beside us, and I looked her dead in the face as she tilted her head. She was gorgeous. Baby was flawless in all aspects, but her soul was ugly.

"We don't have anything else to say to each other, K."

"Maybe you don't have anything else to say, but I have plenty, Wylde."

Leaning forward, I put the blunt in the ashtray and gave her my attention.

"Speak yo' piece. After this, shit is dead."

"How can you be so cold? Do I not mean anything to you?"

"How many times we gotta keep having the same fucking

conversation?" I questioned. "What part of this is so hard for you to fucking understand?"

"The part where you forgot who we are to each other!" Hurt laced her tone and flickered behind her stare. "It was one thing when you chose Billie. I get it. I pushed you too far when I was telling everyone that we were going to be married one day. You don't like anyone making decisions for you."

"Yet, here you are again, with my father, trying to decide my life for me, K. You still ain't learned ya fucking lesson, ma."

"I can't help that I think we belong together. You all but said it yourself when we were together."

"Things change. So do people and situations. I said a lot of shit back then. I believed it too. My pops drilled it into my head. You have to be successful in whatever you do, hold your head, and marry a bad bitch. I used to think him and my mama was the perfect couple. Then she got sick, and I saw up close that he was really a selfish ass bastard. You were there. You saw her getting sicker, weaker, and where was he? Hmm?" My brows dipped, creasing my forehead. "The same shit he did to her, I did with Shayne. I used you, K. I was hurt, and I didn't want to feel that shit. That's all it was. The love I had for you, its not how you think or what you deserve."

"So, that's it?" she pried. "You drop me for a bitch you barely know with two kids. What kind of shit is that? How am I supposed to walk away when I know you're making the wrong choice?"

Scoffing, I shook my head and swept my fingers through my beard.

"And you still don't fucking get it. You need a neon sign or for me to hire somebody to write it across the fucking sky? I don't want you! Pack your shit and go home! We done! Don't call me, don't reach out, don't even ask my fucking father about me, K! You come back around me, and you won't like how I react. You know how I give it up. I might have tamed that beast years ago, but he's still in there. I'm trying not to unleash on anybody that don't deserve it. Don't put yourself on my radar," I warned, not bothering to take in her shocked expression as I stood and moved across the room to the bar.

Wood was tossing back another shot of tequila when I appeared at his side, asking for one my damn self.

"Keep that bitch away from me," I mumbled, tossing my glass back and swallowing the warm drink. "I need to take a piss."

The hallway leading to the bathrooms had low lighting. I could make out shadows amongst the red beams, but the faces weren't exactly clear. I knew it was Waker and Rich speaking as I approached. The discussion between them seemed to be very heated. So much that neither was paying attention to anything else around them.

"Why did you even come here? You thought because I was overseas that you could swoop in?"

"This is my family too, Rich. Or did you forget that little tidbit of information?" my pops challenged.

"It's your family when it's convenient for you, Waker. Keep it a buck. The only person you ever gave a fuck about was yourself," Rich accused.

"Says the fucking golden child." Waker chuckled. "Mama and Daddy ain't here to prop you up no more. Mr. Can Do No Wrong ain't got nobody in his corner. Not even his biggest fan." There was taunting in his tone, and I watched Rich snatch his collar and pin him to a nearby wall.

His octave had lowered significantly, so I had to strain my ears to listen. I wasn't sure what this was about, but the shit had my mind spinning. I knew there was tension between my uncle and father; always had been. Growing up, Rich only came around on holidays, but I loved my uncle to death, and he always made sure to show me love on my birthday. Some of the best gifts I ever got were from him, and some of the most memorable. My own father didn't care what I liked or was into. When he bought me things, it was for something he thought I should be doing. There was no room for anything else with him.

"You should tread fucking lightly, Waker. Your sons already barely respect you. How you think they would feel if they knew the kind of fuck nigga you really are?"

"And what the fuck does that make you, Rich, hmm?" Waker smiled, and my uncle released him before pinching the tip of his nose and adjusting his blazer on his arms and shoulders. "You ain't no better, muthafucka, 'cause you walking around with bones as big as a dinosaur in your closet too. I might not be shit, but guess what, I don't pretend to be anything else. Now, if you want things to remain cohesive within the family, I suggest you let Wylde know that you are implementing some changes. I want to be in charge of the business on the East Coast. Wylde will play second to me."

"Why? So you can attempt to run another business into the ground?" Rich mocked. "Let Wylde and Wood do what they are doing. I'll give you some money, and you can go back to LA and live your fucking life. Nobody wants you here."

"Fuck that! I'm a Katri! I have just as much rights here as any of you mothafuckas! That's my business too, and I want to help run it."

"They don't need fucking help! That's what I'm telling you. You would just be in the way. They are both thriving here."

"You mean without me? That's what this is. Just like everything else, you want to take my boys from me. You tried that before, Rich, remember? Look where that got you." Waker spoke up.

I was so confused about that conversation. What the fuck were they talking about? I kept thinking I was missing something because none of it was making sense other than the fact that Waker seemed to have something over Rich, and he was willing to let him run with it and comply with his requests. He had me fucked up if he thought I was bowing down to anything with Waker, though. The nigga had singlehandedly run our West Coast company into the ground. He was taking money, embezzling, gambling, and had clients turning on us left and right. It cost a lot of money for me to settle and make things right with people on top of making sure that I could rebuild our name into something trustworthy.

"You a fucked up ass person, you know that, Waker?"

"I'm fucked up?" my father questioned, bringing a hand against his chest. "Oh, big brother, you want to talk about you and all your little fucked up ways? No, that's right, you made amends a long time ago, right? You don't feel shit? The one time you couldn't have what you wanted, you couldn't take it, could you? I bet that shit still eats you up to this day, don't it?"

"Fuck you!" Rich spat, which only made Waker cackle.

It was the most venomous I had ever seen or heard him. He was usually the epitome of zen and all that other tranquil shit, but my father had the ability to trigger rage in just about anyone, so I understood.

"Everybody always thought you were the better man. Good thing our parents kept your lack of loyalty within the family."

"You think because you got married and had a family that it makes you better? Let's not forget how you acted like a little bitch, and that's the only reason you gained any of it. Mothafuckas felt sorry for you, Waker. You weak. You can't do shit on your own. You been skating off our name for years, and you don't do shit but make us look bad. You the family member we try to keep hidden, an embarrassment to the Katri name. Even your wife knew it." Rich was smug with his last statement, and I caught the flicker of fury behind Waker's eyes. When he went to swing, Rich reacted first, bopping him in the face with a closed fist that sent Waker falling against the wall.

"You do what you want to do. Wylde and Wood will continue to run things as they have been. If you have a problem with it, I suggest you find your own fucking solution." Rich turned, and I ducked into the nearby bathroom before he could see me.

I heard his footsteps pass as Waker remained in the hallway enraged, punching the wall like an unhinged man. *What the fuck?*

Lishan

"Okay, see the night started a little rocky, but look where we are!" I threw my arms up and popped my ass back as the DJ spun some Latto, and the club gyrated and rapped along to the southern lyrics. Shayne was actually smiling as she twerked with me and threw her head back as the beat carried her away.

"Girl, this was much needed. Wood gon' be mad because we 'bout to become weekend regulars." Sticking her tongue out, she did a spin, and right behind her was this big, lanky ass nigga, licking his lips and admiring her as she moved.

Shayne turned toward me, ignoring his intrusive stare, and shaking her head. He damn sure didn't want a problem because Wylde was more than likely somewhere with eyes all over her.

"We have to drop these babies first," I reminded her, getting winded.

Beginning to fan myself to dry the little beads of sweat gathering at my chest, I started checking around because I needed something to drink. We had danced for at least three songs, so a bitch was parched.

"Come on. Let's go to the bar. I want some juice or something."

"Girl, we are reduced to juice in the club." Shayne tittered.

"My feet hurt. I just want to go home, eat until my stomach feels like it's going to explode, and take a hot bath or shower."

"Damn, why did that just excite me?" I mocked, leading her across the dancefloor to the bar.

"Girl, because we pregnant, in love, and have families to take care of. This was fun, though, and needed. It's been a while since I've been able to go out and actually have a good time. I feel like I already have a lifetime of testimonials to give."

"Who you telling? Folks wouldn't believe half the shit I've been through, and I can't even legally get a drink."

We neared the bar together, and Shayne ordered a Ginger beer while I had pink lemonade. For a few minutes, we sat there chatting. Glancing up, I saw Wylde and Wood hovering over the balcony, eyes on us. That bitch Noemi came up and said something to Wood in his ear. He nodded, and she walked off, then Wood said something to Wylde, and they both disappeared. A moment later, they came down to the bottom level together, and I glanced to see some movement on the stage. Tonight, there was just a DJ set up, and behind him was a big projector screen. I peeped D walking up on the stage, and Noemi lingering beside it with pride across her face as he addressed the crowd.

"I hope everyone is having a good time tonight! We appreciate all of you coming out for the grand reopening of Prized Package."

The crowd clapped and cheered as a large grin fell on his sexy ass face. Knowing that he was all mine only made my heart swell more.

"I want to introduce my partner to everyone. Some of you might remember him. He damn sure knows how to leave an impression. I've known this nigga since we were practically kids, and I couldn't ask for a better mothafucka to help me run shit. So, let's give a welcome to Woodrow Katri!" D waved an arm toward the stage where Wood was stepping up.

I cupped my mouth and screamed my man's name while waving excitedly to him.

This was the first time Wood had ever been in a relationship from what he told me, and it was changing him for the better as far as I was concerned. When we first met, the nigga had a severe aversion to intimacy. Somehow, with me, he was able to lower all those walls he kept up and let me in little by little. Wood and D dapped each other up and quickly embraced while Noemi eyed them both from the side.

"Now, since Wood is part of the family here now, I thought we would give him a proper introduction. I got a few associates here who wanted to assist with that. Yo, come on out, homie!"

Everyone started to look around curiously, and from the opposite side of the stage, a man's shadow moved. That bitch ass nigga Merlin suddenly strolled out with a bitch behind him wearing a short dress, showing off her thick ass thighs. At first, I thought I had to be tripping. My heart thudded as my lips parted and Yeva waved to the crowd while strutting after him with pride.

"The fuck is this?" I asked, looking toward Shayne.

She didn't know either of them, so confusion had set in on her face as her brows came together.

"What's going on? Who is that?" she asked.

"That's Merlin and my snake ass cousin, Yeva. The fuck is she doing with him?"

"I don't know, but Wood looks like he wants to kill everybody up there," Shayne observed.

She was right. There was a murderous glare as his jaw

twitched while D, Merlin, Noemi, and Yeva all seemed amused by the situation.

"The fuck are you doing?" I heard Wood hiss into the mic.

"Wait. Roll the tape!" D shouted.

As soon as I heard the Webbie song playing, my heart sank. Closing my eyes, I lowered my head in shame, not wanting to witness what came next. The crowd was going crazy, yelling and laughing as the video played of me dancing for Merlin during my audition.

"No, the fuck he didn't." Shayne hopped off her bar chair and was about to start toward the stage, enraged, when she was strong armed by Wylde. I didn't know where he had come from, but on stage, Wood had stepped to D and snatched him up in the expensive suit he was draped in.

"The fuck is wrong with you?" He swung and knocked D across the stage with one punch.

Wylde rushed past Shayne to the booth where they were running the video and snatched the DJ out of his chair. He started pushing buttons on the computer until the screen went blank. Wood continued to whup D's ass while Noemi tried to jump in. Wylde charged the stage, tossing that bitch like a doll, and sending her sliding across the floor on her ass while Wood delivered blow after blow to D's face and body. Merlin thought he was going to run up and intervene, but Wylde whirled on him like an animal. When Merlin went for his pistol on his hip, Wylde had already drawn on him, causing the crowd to hiss in unison and fall back from the stage.

"This shit is over. Everybody get the fuck out!" Wylde's growl bounced off the high ceilings, and folks started scrambling over each other to get to the exits.

Security was moving around, helping people to the doors.

"Wood, stop!" Noemi was back on her feet rushing toward him as he finally let up on D and let his limp body fall to the stage. I couldn't even tell if he was breathing. His face was so mangled and bloody now as Wood stood over him, panting while his chest rose heavily.

"Oh shit, D!" Kneeling at his side, Noemi tried to urge him awake, but the only sound that came from him was coughing noises as he choked on his own blood and his body shifted onto his side.

"You could have killed him!" she had the audacity to scream.

"It's still early." Wood wiped the side of his mouth with the back of his hand as Wylde swung his pistol across Merlin's face so hard, I heard that shit from where I was still seated as his face cracked.

His bitch ass hit the stage right beside D. Wylde had put him to sleep, and aimed his pistol at Yeva.

"Get on your knees next to him," Wylde told her.

"What? I'm not—"

Pow!

The shot that whizzed past her head, missing her by barely an inch caused her to flinch as she dropped to her knees like she was told.

"Lock all the doors," Wood ordered security. "Wylde, call Bentley and tell him to bring the truck around. Make sure Shayne and Lis get home safely."

"I'm not leaving." I finally hopped off my chair. "Yeva, the fuck are you doing with him? How could you do this to me? We're supposed to be fucking family."

"Lishan, you know the only thing I'm loyal to is my fucking bag. You left Merlin on stuck. He made me an offer I couldn't refuse," she explained.

"Stupid bitch." I shook my head as Wood walked down the steps from the stage and approached.

"I can't have no loose ends, shorty. I know she your people—"

"Fuck her." My words surprised him, sending both of his brows up. "Handle that."

"Bentley is coming up the alley now." Wylde put us all on notice as Wood leaned in to gently peck my lips.

"We might be a while. Why don't you just go stay at the house with Shayne tonight instead of going home?"

"Okay." I nodded in agreement, and he brought me into an embrace, locking an arm behind my neck and keeping me close.

"This shit ain't on you, shorty. I will never hold this against you either. It is what it is, and this shit ain't gon' make or break you. You hear me?"

"I hear you," I muttered, even though a large part of me wanted to cry right there.

I couldn't allow Yeva or that bitch Noemi to see me like this. That tape was always going to be a part of me. There was nothing I could do about it. I wasn't going to allow it to determine the rest of my life or my worth, though. I did what I had to do to provide for me and my family. If I had to, I would do the shit again. It was Merlin who was in the wrong and took advantage. For that, he was going to pay. Wylde pulled Shayne close and meshed his mouth against hers while resting a hand on her ass.

"Let me know when y'all get home," Wylde instructed.

"Let's go girl." She looped her arm through mine once they parted, and we started toward the back of the club.

"Lishan, the fuck. Where you going? You just leaving me here?" Yeva's voice quaked in fear, but I didn't bother to turn and give her another ounce of my attention.

She made her choice, and it wasn't me. Now she would have to live with the repercussions. Bentley had the truck waiting for us right at the door. He opened the back door, and

Shayne and I climbed inside. My gaze was lost out of the window as the truck shifted gears, and we pulled away from the club. Shayne scooted closer to me, draping an arm over my shoulders, and pulling me in.

"Leave that shit where it is, sis," she advised softly. "That is your past. That's not your family, but I am. I will always be here for you, Lis."

Her words brought tears to my eyes that I finally let fall as I rested my head against her. The shit comforted me in a way I hadn't expected. Looking into Shayne's face, I believed her. She had no reason to fake me. She didn't know me from a can of paint out here and she took a chance and put me on in the office. I fucked up when she first hired me, but it didn't hinder her from teaching me. She didn't criticize. Instead, she gave me the game and encouraged me. Back then, I didn't know her patience came from having kids, but I should have picked up on it.

Much like me, Shayne was a nurturer. She wasn't as spicy as I was, but she was damn sure a rider. Sometimes she was timid and stood in her own way, in my opinion, but I could see that fierceness in her when it came to those she cared about.

Once we arrived back at the house, we both kicked our shoes off and tossed them to the side. The TV sounds from the living room drew us both to the doorway. The four pack was spread out on the floor in their own sleeping bags while ESPN danced across the screen. They were out cold, but Nael had his feet propped up on the coffee table while chewing kernels of popcorn. When he caught us lingering in the doorway, he sat up and studied us closely.

"Aye. I didn't know y'all was back. Did you have a good time?" He set the medium sized bowl on the table.

"For the most part," I muttered.

"I'm starving." Shayne rubbed her stomach and moved

down the hall toward the kitchen. I was right behind her with the same sentiments.

She went to the refrigerator and started pulling containers out before going to the cabinet and grabbing plates. I eased up onto a bar chair and propped an elbow on the counter as I placed my chin in my hand and watched her move around in that elaborate ass gown while making sure we had something to eat.

"What were your parents like?" I questioned, realizing I didn't know a lot about her life before she came to Greenwich.

Shayne paused and brought the bowls to the counter. There was a deep dish pizza for us to indulge in. She also brought out a container of cookie dough ice cream as she stacked our plates with food.

"Well, my mama was a homemaker. She did all the ordinary housewife shit. She had her little hustles on the side, she sewed and did custom uniforms for a lot of the local sports teams that we sponsored, along with the rest of our community. I really had a low key, normal life growing up. My daddy owned a chop shop. He serviced just about any and everybody. When I was little, he would come and go. I guess I never really thought about it until now, but he moved around without us a lot. My mama said he had business all over the country. He was getting parts from all over, taking freelance gigs to repair certain models that required his expertise. It paid good and took care of us. I don't remember ever struggling like that."

"Sounds ideal," I kidded, and Shayne went to take one of the plates to the microwave.

"Maybe." She put it on two and a half minutes and came back to join me. "It wasn't always perfect. My parents fought and my brother and I didn't always get along, especially after I met Elim." She gave an eyeroll. "Everything seemed like a fight to the point that I was alienated from everyone I loved. He wanted me to focus solely on him. I thought that was how it was supposed to be when you were in love." She gave a shrug. "Why are we talking about this again?" Frowning, Shayne perked up as the timer on the microwave went off.

She grabbed the second plate, went to get the warm one, and traded them out. After snatching a fork from the dishrack, she walked everything over to me and set it down.

"I don't know. I had a conversation with my grandpa the other day and Myra. Merlin's mama." I grabbed a fork, said a quick prayer, and dug into the dish. "Apparently, my mama knew who my daddy was and never said anything to anybody. Not even to him."

"What? So, your daddy never knew about you?" Shayne pried.

"Nope." I shook my head and took another mouthful.

It was so light and flavorful that I wanted to savor it. Shayne grabbed a spoon and took the lid off the carton of ice cream. Dunking it inside, she brought a large spoonful to her lips.

"Damn, that's crazy."

"I don't know where I would be if I hadn't met Wood. He's been a blessing." Thinking back to our first encounter when he walked into the building, I couldn't help but smile.

He was flirting out the gate. I told myself I wouldn't get lost in his warm brown eyes, or that boyish smile, but he had me the minute he opened his mouth and licked his lips. My heart fluttered, and the nigga had me stuttering, so I should have known he was going to fuck up my life. At that moment in time, I had no idea the kind of impact he'd have. I prayed that whatever he had to do tonight didn't change who he was or who he was becoming because I realized in this cold world, a man like Woodrow Katri was very much needed.

Chapter 9
Wood

"Wake up, nigga!" I kicked the chair where D was strapped down while circling him like my prey.

His body jolted as he lifted his chin from his chest. Both eyes were nearly sealed shut, but he managed to peel one open and take me in as I paused in front of him. I had taken off the formal attire and stood in just my slacks and white beater as he came to. I typically wasn't a violent nigga unless provoked. It had been a long time since I'd had to put those skills to use. Wylde and I ran one of the most lucrative gun rings in the states as well, but you would never know it because we barely touched that side of the business.

My brother and I prided ourselves on being legit and running a company that stood for something. Having Katri Realty and Development gave us something legitimate to build on as well. Before, I didn't think either of us thought about leaving anything behind for anyone. Now, it seemed we both had a legacy we were building on. I was thinking about the future and my baby with Lishan every other second of each day. When you out here doing things for yourself its one thing, but carrying the weight of an entire family on your shoulders was something else completely.

"The fuck you doing, Wood?" D grumbled in agony.

Nigga's jaw and mouth was so fucked up that it all came out a little garbled as he twitched in his chair and tried to get out of the ropes that bound his hands together.

"You had to have a fucking death wish with the stunt you pulled tonight." Pacing with a machete in my hand, I tapped the sharp blade against the palm of the opposite hand.

"That wasn't on me. That mothafucka Merlin set this up. Him and that bitch he was with!" D spat, and then he spit blood onto the floor beside his chair.

He could leave his DNA all over this muthafucka. This spot was where we tortured niggas like him. It would be wiped down when we were done like we were never even there. I had some of the best crime scene cleaners in the business working for me. Grabbing the back of his neck, I jerked him forward and made sure he was looking into my eyes. Only one of his was taking me in, bouncing across my face fearfully as he tried to keep it open. His mouth was twisted, lip all busted up and swollen from the beating I had given him.

"I'll deal with them. We talking about you and your bitch. You got any last words, Noemi?" I glanced to his left.

She was just coming to as her eyes flickered and then stretched when she realized she was bound to a chair similar to her man's.

Becoming unhinged, she started rocking and trying to break free in the chair, but I was sure she wasn't getting out of anything.

"Wood, please, don't do this," she pleaded. "Please. There are things that you don't know."

"You did this, No. Remember that when this is over. You

had the chance to do right, but you chose to go along with this bullshit, knowing it wouldn't go well for you."

"You doing all this over that little stripper bitch!" D shrieked.

Raising my hand, I smacked him across the face. More blood spewed from his mouth as his head dropped to one side. Noemi whimpered as D lifted his head.

"Nah, don't cry now, bitch." I shook my head as she trembled in her seat. "Now, answer me this, D. The fuck did you think was going to happen when you pulled this shit? Did you think I was gon' laugh it off or think this shit was funny?"

"It was a fucking joke, that's it," he argued.

"Nah, I don't think it was." I paused and studied the blade against my hand. "See, my memory is full of all kinds of little details. You been capping since high school. Nigga always wanted to fit in, be down, and act like he was part of the clique. You remember that, bro?" Over my shoulder, I addressed my brother as he leaned against a metal table with his arms crossed in front of him.

He had been rather calm and quiet during all this, with a fresh blunt resting between his fingers. He took a deep pull, allowing the smoke to fill his lungs before exhaling and squinting through the clouds floating around him.

"Yeah, I remember that fuck nigga. He was corny and always following you around and shit. Used to try to dress like you and talk like you and everything. Didn't he make the B team on basketball too?" Wylde chuckled as a dark glare filled D's gaze.

"Yeah, that nigga. No originality. Even now. You had to go and get a bitch you knew I fucked with, so you could feel like you was on my level. Ain't that right?"

"Fuck you!" he managed to yell. "You blew back into town, thinking you still had it like that, trying to check my soldiers,

but I run this shit now! You left, and niggas forgot about you!"
He let a smug grin spread over his face, which I knocked off
with a fist.

The chair almost tipped over because I had hit him so hard.
I was done talking to this nigga. There was no reason for me to
interrogate him when it was all plain and simple. He did all this
shit in an attempt to get back at me for his inadequacies. It was
jealousy and envy 101.

"Yeah, you don't like hearing the truth. You sure that baby
she carrying is really yours? From what Merlin told me, nigga
been fucking her on a regular since she was seventeen years
old. That ain't yo' bitch. She for the fucking streets."

"You one to talk." I waved the machete toward Noemi.

I didn't believe shit he had to say about Lishan. Merlin was
a bitch nigga and would say or do anything to make her
look bad.

"You fucking on the neighborhood hoe and got the nerve to
come for my girl. And let's be real. Niggas ain't never forgot
about me. They know how I give it up, and when I'm done with
you, all that will be reinstated. Niggas like you be under the
delusion that they run something. Whole time, niggas just be
biding they time until they can take your spot. Nobody knows
that better than me, D. You fucked up. Now this club belongs
to me."

"You kill me, and my crew is coming hard behind that." He
gritted his teeth.

"It's a chance I'm willing to take." Giving a shrug, I lifted
the machete and used it to chop into his flesh, dismembering
one of his hands from his body.

When I was done with him, I had one of the guards box
him up and load him into a barrel so he could be disposed of
properly. There wasn't going to be any evidence this nigga even
existed when we were done with him.

"What you want to do with her?" Wylde bobbed his head toward Noemi once they had taken all the contents of D's body from the room.

With my head down, I was still covered in blood while taking in a few breaths. Bringing my eyes up, they locked on my brother as he leaned against the metal frame of the door.

"Take her ass to the pines. That bitch Yeva too. Make it look like a drunk driving accident."

Nodding, Wylde called to one of our men over his shoulder and they came in and untied Noemi. She fought and screamed the entire time until one of them knocked her the fuck out so they could drag her out back. I was numb. The pines was a heavily wooded area that had been known to hold bodies over the years. Shit was so thick it was usually hard to find anything. It rained a lot in the area too, so it was always washing shit away, making it the perfect place to dump a body. The river wasn't far, and the roads were so narrow and tight that it wasn't shit for you to get lost or lose sight and veer off into the water.

I didn't have as much rage left for Noemi in all this. Given that we had a relationship at one point, I thought maybe I should be the one to end her, but it didn't matter to me one way or another. I had spent enough energy on D and still had this nigga Merlin to deal with. Yeva was another story. I didn't know that bitch, but she had crossed Lishan and was supposed to be her blood, so that was enough for me.

"Bring that nigga in here," I ordered.

Seconds later, Merlin was dragged in, feet scraping against the concrete floor as his chin touched his chest. He was placed in a chair but remained slumped over. Lifting my head to the sky, I took in a deep breath before I spun to face him. The only sound in the room was the drip from the sink over in the corner. It was kind of comforting, so I didn't bother to adjust it. Wylde hovered in the doorway and glanced in my direction.

"You good?" he checked with me.

"I'm good." I gave him a nod, and he grabbed the knob to the door and backed out of the room while closing it.

"Wake up, player!" Smacking his cheek repeatedly caused Merlin to stir.

His eye was turning black and blue, and he rocked a fresh lump on the forehead from Wylde knocking him out.

"The fuck? Where am I?" He shook off the discombobulation and went right to anger.

"Shit, you in the place you go right before you die. Whatever the fuck that is." I chuckled, and his dark eyes latched onto mine with hate.

"That little pussy got you tight." Merlin snickered, and one fist balled into the palm of my other hand. "I get it, though. She got it. That's a money maker right there. I knew it from the first time she let me hit."

"You one of them hoe ass, raised by ya mama, daddy was a bitch nigga, ass niggas. A womanizer. Nigga always in his feelings about the past and blaming everybody else for his shortcomings. The type to rule with fear, no respect for nobody, think the world owes yo' weak ass something. You a fucking coward that hides behind women. You exploit them, demean and belittle them, and you enjoy it. That's the part that's gon' get you fucked off." I wagged a finger at him as I took a couple steps back.

"And what are you? Hmm? D told me you ran through bitches around here too. His girl was one of 'em. You the nigga that ran to the West Coast when shit got real while everybody else got locked up," Merlin revealed.

There was dead air between us that suddenly thickened. Smiling with a self-assured nod, he tittered a bit.

"Yeah. I heard all about it. They saying you the one that snitched and sent Glory to prison."

"Is that right?" I mocked, tapping my chin and nodding before I started to walk around the room.

We were in an abandoned garage on the outskirts of the city, surrounded by nothing but industrial buildings and trees beyond them and in between. The next mothafucka was so far away they wouldn't hear him or anybody scream, even if this place wasn't soundproof.

"Yeah. You talking about a bitch nigga and womanizing like you ain't been that nigga. At least I stand on mine. Fuck these bitches, and that includes my hoe ass mama," he growled. "She ain't never did shit for me but put me on to how these hoes really operate. I make money with her, so I keep her around as a business partner, but I don't trust her ass as far as I can throw her. You a stupid mothafucka if you don't think Lishan ain't the same. All women are. They lie, they sneaky, they manipulative, and then turn around and want to be respected. Fuck that and fuck them! They all got a price!" he ranted, looking crazy as hell, practically foaming at the mouth he was so turned up.

It was in that very moment that I knew I was doing the right thing. This was the kind of energy this world didn't need. He wasn't going to just go away. As long as he was around, he was a threat that I could not tolerate. That turn that other cheek shit didn't apply here.

"You sound mad hurt, my nigga. Yo' mama didn't love you, so you decided to take it out on all the other women in the world."

"I put money in the pockets of most of these bitches. I'm the reason they got food on the table, bills is paid, and they kids can walk around in fresh gear. Lishan acted like she was too good for a nigga to put her on or something. That's why I dealt with her how I did and gave her the bare minimum. If she couldn't fall in line, then she couldn't eat like the rest of my obedient hoes. Yeva knew what was up, that's why she jumped on the team. It was only a matter of time before Lishan came around. Until she started working for you. Fuck these bitches. My job as a man is to keep these hoes in check if nobody else do. A nigga like me brings balance to the world," he concluded cockily.

"Time to tip the scale then, homie." Coming up behind him with the machete that I had quietly grabbed from the table, I placed a hand against his forehead and jerked his head toward my stomach. Taking the blade, I sliced it across his throat, and his warm blood coated my fingers. The gurgling noises were comforting as he fought for air. Closing my eyes, I took in a few deep breaths while listening to him as he gasped, and then everything grew still except that little drip from the faucet.

A couple of hours later, after discarding my bloody clothes, I cleaned myself up and rode with Wylde back to Shayne's to call it a night. The ride was quiet between me and my brother. We shared a blunt and had a couple of shots on the way there. By the time we arrived, I was lit. After taking another shower and changing once I touched down, I climbed onto the pillowtop mattress with my girl.

"What time is it?" Lishan rubbed sleep from her eyes in the guest bedroom of Shayne's house.

"Time for some sleep, shorty." I kissed the nape of her neck as she moved her ass closer to my dick and rested it there.

Her warm, soft frame against me was home to a nigga, no matter where we were. It was crazy how she had swept in and switched everything up. I was just going with it because she was cool and collected most of the time. She was young, but she didn't let you see her sweat like that. If she didn't know something, she asked, and she soaked up the game I was giving her. Most chicks already thought they knew everything. Lishan was still teachable, and that was more valuable than most mothafuckas realized.

"You know what I've been thinking about?" she asked as I closed my eyes and inhaled her scent.

"What's that?"

"How not everybody in my position ever comes across someone who genuinely cares about them. You might be a rude ass nigga, but you got heart, Wood. You go hard when you care. You've done more for me and my family in a few months than anyone has ever done for us in life. We got family out there, but they disconnected from my mama so long ago that they discarded us too. Misael was the only one who stepped up so we wouldn't go into the system. Now, everything is on me."

"Nah, it ain't." I shook my head. "And as long as a nigga breathing, it never will be. You solid, Lis. You look out for your family. You do that shit because it's what you supposed to do too. You know how many people would have said fuck it and just did them in your position? You took the hard route. You could have easily thought about yourself and that's it, but you sacrificed so your brothers and sister didn't have to. For that, you deserve it all. I don't give a fuck what you had to do to make it happen."

She turned to face me, a smile on her face as her eyes misted.

"I know what I want to do now. I want to open transitional housing for families. I want to buy the blocks we grew up on and turn them into something nice. Not like how we were living. We'll provide food, shelter, and transportation like shuttles to get people from appointments, and even get the kids to and from school. I want a rec center too, something to replace the old one they shut down years ago. Those kids need somewhere to go after school, and we need to bring back the youth sports teams and get involved. What do you think?"

"I think you got it, shorty. You got the vision, and I got the money to put behind it. Get some sleep."

Shayne

The door to my bedroom creaked open, and I immediately sat up on the side as Wylde's shadow moved across the wall. Tossing the covers to the side, I rushed to him and threw my arms around him, damn near knocking the wind from him.

"Damn, mama." His arms fell around me and held me firmly against his chest.

"It's late. I thought something had happened." I finally let go and pulled back to look him over. I was feeling all over his chest and his defined abs, making sure he was fine.

"I'm good, Shayne," he assured me. "It's almost six in the morning, though. What you doing up?"

"I couldn't sleep, worried about you. I tossed and turned all over the bed."

"You need to rest, baby." He rested a hand across my stomach and lowered his chin so he could peer into my eyes.

"I will, now that you're here." Standing on my toes in nothing but my boy shorts and a wife beater, I meshed my lips into his.

His hand landed against the side of my face, pulling me closer and deepening the exchange with his tongue. My nipples tingled, counteracting with the rapid thumping between my legs as he cuffed one side of my ass. Reaching for his pants, I undid them and took backward steps toward the bed, pulling him along with me until I lowered myself onto my back against the mattress, and he was hovering over me.

"I missed you," I whispered, eyes bouncing off his as the moonlight illuminated the bedroom.

"Yeah?" Wylde's lips caressed my neck, assaulting it as he nibbled on my earlobe and brushed my hair to one side so he could access the back of my ear.

"How much?"

It was a sensitive spot for me, especially when he was inside me.

"Mmm. So much." Soft moans fell from my lips as his hard body lowered onto mine.

His touch was soft as his big hands roamed my body, sending serious, soul stirring tremors over me. My back arched as his lips brushed my collar bone, and he applied tongue and lips against my flesh. It seemed like forever since this type of pleasure had absorbed me. Tugging at each side of my boy shorts, Wylde pulled them past my thighs and down to my ankles before he started to plant slow kisses up them as his fingertips also grazed me.

"Turn over," he ordered, sending my heart into palpitations from his deep baritone.

Pulling the wife beater over my head, he plucked one of my erect nipples between his thumb and first finger. With my back perfectly arched, I awaited his next move. I was anxious to have him inside me again as his thick rod swung between his legs. His mouth latched onto my pussy, nearly sucking my soul through it as I juiced up and my mouth parted in bliss. Nipping my teeth at my bottom lip, I held back the scream that wanted to erupt and instead grabbed a handful of sheets as his expert tongue licked and flicked along my juicy pearl.

"Fuckkkk, Wylde!" I groaned, feeling my orgasm knocking as my stomach clenched with every flick.

Sticking one finger inside, then another, he tapped at my spot and sent a wave of warmth over me as I came. He kissed along each cheek before traveling up my spine and tapping his thick mushroom head against my dripping center. With his fingers digging into my hips on either side, Wylde plunged inside me until he hit bottom, and I felt his balls bounce against my ass.

"Shit!" he grunted, leaving his dick in place, throbbing inside of me.

He pulled back and hit me with strokes so deep I swear the nigga was in my guts. As if he was punishing me, he tapped harder, knocking the fucking coins out with each thrust he delivered.

"Wylde!" I couldn't fight him.

Instead, I matched his energy and threw my back into it as his thick rod lined my walls over and over again.

"I feel it, mama. Bust that shit down for me," he encouraged, hips grinding in circular motions while he went deeper, sending me over the edge as he coaxed me to my peak.

"Fuck!"

I threw my ass back, taking every inch and coating his dick until it jerked inside me, and his nut spilled out. I rocked on the tip until I was sure he had dumped every drop into my womb, and we collapsed in bed. With a heaving chest, Wylde fell on his back beside me. There was sweat coating us as his penetrating orbs latched onto mine. He reached for my hand, intertwined our fingers, and pulled me closer. Throwing one leg across his middle section, I accepted his smooth hand against my thigh as his supple lips pressed against my shoulder.

I didn't remember drifting off, but the sound of his rapid heartbeat lulled me to sleep. The following morning, the sunlight peeking through the blinds sent me rolling over to my side in an empty bed. Inhaling, the aroma of bacon and sausage rumbled my stomach. Still naked, with just the sheets draped over me, I sat up and peered around the room. There was no sign of Wylde as I went to brush my teeth and use the bathroom. Once I washed my face and moisturized it, I could no longer take my stomach growling, so I headed downstairs. Bypassing the bedrooms of the kids, I saw that they were all still sleeping soundly.

Nearing the bottom of the staircase, I listened as Nael and Wylde's voices carried down the hallway.

"So, you listened in on a private conversation, and now you ready to blow everybody's life up?" Nael questioned, his tone harsher than I'd ever heard, especially with Wylde.

For the most part, they seemed to get along really well. My uncle respected him and vice versa. I couldn't help but pause in stride and listen with my back against the wall so they wouldn't see me eavesdropping.

"You don't think they deserve to know?" Wylde pried.

"What good is it going to do anybody?" Nael shot back in a raised whisper. "Both of those girls been through enough."

"That's why you have to tell them. The fact that Shayne is even here should be a sign."

"A sign?" Nael scoffed. "A sign of what?"

"I don't know. Something brought her here. At first it was this job at Katri, then she met Lishan and hired her. Now they best fucking friends and don't even know the half of it. Shit ain't right, and you know it. What would Miles do?"

"Deserve to know what?" I asked, stepping into the kitchen with a lifted brow.

Both men's attention darted toward me, and Wylde straightened up at the counter opposite my uncle, who was making plates. He shot a warning glare at Wylde as he scooped the last of the eggs onto a plate.

"What are you two in here talking about, and what does it have to do with me?" I stepped closer to the counter, arms tucked across my chest while waiting for an answer.

"What's going on? It smells so good in here." Lishan strolled in with Wood not far behind her, yawning and running his hand over his sponge top while his other one anxiously circled his stomach.

"Hell yeah. Point me in the direction of the swine." They

both grabbed plates, but I was far from letting this conversation slide.

"Why y'all looking like that?" Lishan plucked a piece of bacon from her plate and took a bite.

"Nael, what are you hiding, and why don't you want Wylde to tell me?" I prodded.

"Because it's not mine or Wylde's information to tell," Nael pointed out. "Your father ain't here to tell it either."

"What does Daddy have to do with any of this?" I queried, brows knitting together in a frown.

"Wylde overheard a conversation between me and Lishan's grandfather," Nael began, drying his hands on a towel before shaking his head.

"Okay, so what's the big secret? I didn't think you knew her grandfather."

"You know that me, Rich, and your father were all acquainted. When your Pops traveled, sometimes I would tag along with him. We stopped in Greenwich once or twice, just passing through. Occasionally, we would hit up Rich. Anyway, there was this girl..." Nael sighed. "Her name was Leslie."

Lishan nearly choked on her food as she lowered herself onto one of the bar chairs.

"My mama?" she asked after swallowing some orange juice that Wood had poured for her.

"I didn't know her. She and my brother, Miles, they were close," Nael divulged.

"How close?" I prodded, knots forming in my belly as my pulse quickened.

For some reason, all my instincts were screaming as Nael's eyes darkened before lowering. Any questions or uncertainty I had, the answers were buried in his gaze.

"Nael."

"Close." Nael emphasized.

"Wait, so are you saying that her father..." Lishan aimed a finger at me, "and my mother were together? Like together?" she questioned.

"A couple of times," Nael replied. "It was a long time ago."

"I... I don't believe you," I muttered, overwhelmed by the urge to cry as I thought about my daddy stepping out on my mama. Their marriage seemed solid enough, but I knew there were times when they would argue and go through their shit too. I was a kid and didn't pay much attention to it. It typically blew over, and they would make up.

"Shayne—"

"You saying Daddy cheated on Mama, Nael? Is that what you're telling me?" I demanded, noticing the disappointment flitting across his face.

"He loved your mother. There was never a doubt about that. You, Dimi, and her were all that mattered to him. I didn't think anything came of his time with Leslie. According to Misael, it did." My uncle's warm eyes fell on Lishan.

Hers misted as she dropped her fork to her plate and leaned back. The silence that enveloped the room echoed off the walls as alarms rang in my head. This was crazy, and it felt like my mind had literally exploded.

"Oh, my God," Lishan mumbled.

"Misael says that Lishan is Mile's daughter. He never knew about her," he confessed, sending earth shattering news through the room and nearly knocking me off my feet with it.

I grabbed the counter to hold myself up as Lishan and I stared at each other crazily. From day one, we seemed to mesh well. She was always so high spirited and full of optimism. She didn't even have experience, but I took a chance with her based on her personality. Not once had I thought to judge her or ridicule her.

"She's your sister. Your little sister," Nael elaborated.

Disbelief clouded both of our faces, and my eyes stung with fresh tears. It wasn't her fault, but the resentment in my chest was stifling. Doubling over, I held my stomach and took in deep breaths as I tried to hold myself up at the counter. Wylde was at my side, keeping me in a standing position at his side as a well spilled down my cheeks. My father, the man I loved and adored before anyone else had let me down. The worst part was, he wasn't here to give me the answers I needed. That was even more of a gut punch as I tried to grasp the information I had just been given. I had another sibling. A sister, and I didn't know what to do with that.

Yanking away from Wylde, I stomped toward the patio doors. Suffocating, I needed to take in fresh air. Pushing both French doors open, I burst into the crisp day and lifted my head to the sky. The wind against my face caused my tears to dry, but more followed. *How is this happening?* Suddenly, it seemed like everything I thought I knew about my life and my family was a lie, and I found myself questioning so much. After a few minutes of holding the railing wrapped around the terrace so tight that you could see my knuckles, I sighed as footsteps came up behind me.

"Shayne." Lishan's soft voice caused me to take her in over my shoulder as she moved toward me with caution. "I can't imagine what you must be feeling right now."

"No, Lishan, you can't," I agreed, giving her my back.

I didn't want to hold anything against her; I just couldn't help but feel a way. My parents and brother weren't around for me to grill about the situation, and knowing that Nael was content keeping it from me left me disappointed too. I thought he had my back.

"Okay, well, let me give you a glimpse into my mind." She came out to join me. "All the family I have depends on me for everything. Even when my mama was alive, I had to do it all because she was in the streets. She contracted AIDS when I was twelve and died a year later. I always wondered about my daddy, what he was like, and if he had a family or other kids. I tried not to think of it too much because I was blessed to have the family I did. Regardless of what we didn't have, I loved my brothers and sister. Even Misael's mean ass. When I met you, I thought you were so pretty, smart, and talented. You didn't let people walk over you or talk crazy to you either. I looked up to you, and you inspired me. You also took a chance on me when you didn't have to."

Turning so that I faced her, a small smile tugged the corners of my mouth. Although I could harbor acrimony and scream or behave like a child, the truth was, none of this was Lishan's fault. She and I were blameless in this, but we were family at the end of the day. The instant connection that I hadn't given a second thought when we met now made more sense than ever. Those deep, wide set brown eyes were familiar as hell as I thought about the many times I had looked into my father's or even Dimi's.

"This has nothing to do with you, Lis." Lowering my head, I let the tears scorch my eyes while I shut them.

"I know." She came up beside me and stared out at the backyard with me.

"He's not here to talk to, or be mad at... and I want answers, but... I don't want to put this on you. It's not your fault."

"What was he like?" Her tone was so soft, vulnerable as she glanced my way.

"I don't know. Assertive, vocal, proud. He stood for something. If he could help, he would, whether it be time or money. I took that for granted over the years," I admitted as I bowed my head. "You kind of look like him. More than me, kind of like Dimi with the brown skin and those eyes. I looked more like my mama. Everyone called me her twin."

"So," Lishan cleared her throat and avoided my stare. "Misael told me a few things before I knew about all this."

"Things like what?"

"He said that... well, that your mother knew. She paid my mama to leave and never come back."

The revelation rocked my core, damn near gutting me.

Speechless, Lishan and I exchanged a heavy glance before I stood upright and gave the banister my back to lean against. It would be so easy to argue or go against her on this and call her a liar.

"I'm only telling you this because, well, I don't want there to be anything left unsaid between us. If what Nael said is true, we're sisters. Regardless of how it happened, it is what it is. I already love, care about you, and pray for you like I would a blood sister." Tears welled in her eyes.

"Yeah," I agreed and nodded. "It's just... hard. I don't know if you would understand."

"Maybe not. Doesn't mean I can't listen," Lishan said.

"I spent a lot of time unappreciative of my family. Whatever our struggles were, a lot of them came from me being with Elim. The last few years were... strained. I saw them on holidays, talked to them every few months. My kids didn't know them the way grandparents should know their grandkids. I wasted a lot of time being Elim's obedient little baby mama, which caused a rift. I can never get that time back, and now they're all gone." The weight of that broke me down.

I crumbled, legs bending as I wrapped my arms around my knees while pressing my back against the iron railing.

"Maybe this is God's way of giving us both what we need." She knelt beside me and positioned herself identical to me with both knees in the air. "If you think about it, it's all kind of cosmic. You ending up here after all this time, meeting Rich, Wylde, and

Wood. Me working for you. I mean... look how everything aligned. It's right out of some crazy ass novel." She snickered, and I couldn't help but consider her point of view while my gaze got lost ahead.

"I never told you because... it wasn't something I told everyone. Miles is still alive," I revealed. "He's still breathing, but... it's not him lying in that bed. One day, I'm going to have to decide what to do and if I should just pull the plug and let him go. I'm not ready for that yet, though. It's selfish, but... I can't let him go." I shrugged, and she nodded along.

"I get it. Do you think... would it be okay if I saw him?" she timidly questioned.

"It's been a while since I've visited. We could take the drive this week if you want," I suggested.

"I can never replace the family you had, Shayne." Lishan began.

"No," I agreed. "It's not about that either. At the end of the day, we are family. You've been working for me since you were like eighteen. We've had lunch together and spent day in and day out together all this time. Now, it just makes it official." Extending my arm, I grabbed her hand in mine and locked them together.

Giving her a big grin, which she returned, I pulled her into a tight embrace and held her there for the longest. We squeezed each other until neither of us could breathe and Wylde and Wood came strolling out together.

"Y'all done having y'all little after school, Oprah highlights moment?" Wood asked, holding his plate and scooping eggs onto a fork and into his mouth.

"Fuck you!" I flipped him off as Lishan and I stood.

"Should have known y'all crazy, stubborn asses was related." Wood shook his head, and Wylde chortled.

"Aye, be easy on my sister." Lishan rebutted with a grin.

"Sister." I chuckled and tucked some of my hair behind my ear. "Dimitri would have loved this. I stressed him out enough."

Life was constantly showing me that at any given moment, things could take a turn, for better or for worse. I was always waiting for the latter. Lishan had every reason not to, and she was one of the most optimistic people I had ever come across. Once we got back inside, we all sat around at the table, having breakfast together.

With Wylde next to me and my leg draped across his lap as we both smashed the waffles, eggs, and bacon, I simpered at the little flicker of lust burning behind his stare. He was looking at me like he wanted to finish what had happened in the early hours of this morning. The only other man I had ever been with was Elim, and he didn't put it down like that.

Don't get me wrong, I was with the nigga for ten years, so there was chemistry and passion for sure. He was just a different type of lover. With him, it was all aggression all the time. Very few times did I recall lovemaking, and that was very early in the relationship when he was trying to get me to fall for him. Wylde explored my body carefully, taking his time. He seemed to savor the experience just as much as I did when we were tangled in the sheets. He was attentive and always made sure I got mine before he even made an attempt to climax. There were times he was so deep inside me that our souls were bonded, and I wasn't sure who was who because we somehow molded into one. That was intimacy, and it was something that had been lacking for me for a long time.

"So, I thought we could cook dinner tonight here. Shayne, we need to go to the store and grab everything while the kids are asleep. I don't want to hear nothing about them tagging along." Lishan swallowed her orange juice and waved her hand in the air.

"Ah, hell nah. Y'all leaving them here with us?" Wood

asked, falling back in his chair. "Gon' fuck around, and every-body gon' be either locked outside or tied the fuck up. That's too many kids."

"They leaving them here with you." Wylde pointed across the table. "I got something to do. Besides, you Uncle Wood. Everybody loves you. Gives you time to practice before Lishan drops."

"The fuck, Wylde? Who side you on? How you just gon' leave me here with the terror squad?" Wood's face balled up. "And I ain't the only one with a baby on the way," he reminded him.

"Where are you going?" I asked, since this was the first time he'd even mentioned of going anywhere.

"To the office. I got some paperwork I need to pick up. I won't be gone long." Leaning forward, he kissed my lips and rested a hand on my thigh.

Lishan and Wood got up to take our plates to the sink when we were done and then disappeared with him whispering in her ear and smacking her ass. Wylde's hands wandered to my warm clit, and he thumbed it in circle motions while grinning sexily. Now that we had broken that barrier, we were about to wear each other out.

"You trying to take a shower with me before I go?" he toyed with me.

I couldn't resist. It was easy to be addicted to him. We ducked out of the kitchen, and he scooped me into his arms at the bottom of the stairs, then carried me all the way to the bedroom. We locked the door and spent the next twenty minutes steaming up the shower. I was so fulfilled when I got out that a bitch got back in the bed after slipping into my Pink joggers and matching shirt. Wylde kissed me before he left and said he would be back, and I slipped off into dreamland.

Lishan

The following week...

"Wood acts like his ass is eating for two," I complained, digging into my little frozen yogurt container while Shayne and I moved through the mall, toting bags of items we had picked up from the dozens of stores we hit over the span of about three hours. "I can't even eat around him. Nigga always wants some, even when he got his own. He sleeps as much as me too. I swear you would think he was the one carrying life."

"Wylde's ass is suddenly sick as a dog." Shayne snickered and took a mouthful of her yogurt. "I ain't mad at it because I spent weeks like that. I'm finally starting to feel like me again. I can sleep at night, but occasionally, I have a nightmare or two."

"About what?" I wanted to know as we neared the food court so we could take a seat.

My feet and back were on fire from all the damn walking we were doing. Dropping some of the bags at my feet just like Shayne as she pulled out the chair beside me, we both peeped the scene as Bentley hovered in the background, people watching as well.

"Its going to sound ridiculous." She shook her head. "They are about Elim and his mama. They both keep popping up like the grim fucking reaper. You know what the crazy part is? I haven't heard anything from anyone in his family. Nothing. They talked about the shooting and everything and that they found Caterina and Elim dead, but that's it. Not a peep from a member of his family, though."

"Maybe they're just grieving." I shrugged.

"Maybe," she muttered, eyes veering off to the side. "I just don't want to be looking over my shoulder all the time."

"Well, we don't have to worry about that, dealing with the men in our lives. That nigga Wood knows all about my moves.

He thinks he slick, but I know this damn necklace he bought me has a damn tracker in it." I played with the pendant on my chain.

I adored the piece, and it was clearly pricey, but it was how he emphasized that I needed to wear it every day that got me wondering what it was really about.

"Girl, what?" Shayne's brows dipped as she leaned back in her chair and crossed one leg over the other.

We were both pretty casual in just our jeans, graphic tees, and cardigans. She wore her velvet Pumas, and I rocked my Dior sneakers that Wood ordered for me when he got his a couple of weeks ago. It was crazy how our styles were so different, but we were similar in a lot of ways. I noticed little features that we shared every day.

"Yep. He was on this 'you need to wear this shit every day' shit, or at least when you leave the house. Like, nigga."

"When did he give you that?" she questioned, playing with the Pandora bracelet on her wrist.

"Not long ago," I answered.

"Wylde took my bracelet and added new charms to it and gave it to me. He got Storm a necklace with a teddy bear and her birth stone," Shayne responded, a pensive expression on her face as she peered up at me.

"Coincidence?" I lifted my brows and simpered. "I guess we can't be completely pissed off, considering everything that's happened. It's kind of cute."

"And they kinda crazy," Shayne piped up. "You ever wonder why they call him Wylde?"

"Girl, I've seen that glint in his eyes. Nigga might be a tall glass of pretty, but trust me, that beast is in there. You saw how he handled that nigga Merlin. I don't put nothing past him or Wood for that matter." Those Katri brothers were the truth. I got the feeling we had barely scratched the surface with either of them.

"So, you ready for tomorrow?" Shayne questioned.

We had agreed to go and see our father at the facility, and ever since, my nerves had been bouncing around. Over the last week, nothing had changed with us. I realized that our relationship was already solid and organic. I admired her, respected her, and she did the same. She was a few years older too, and since day one, she had never been one to keep any kind of knowledge from me. She was the one who inspired me to go to college. When I graduated, I planned on diving headfirst into things with Myra and Merlin. Working at Katri was an eye-opener, and I realized that I could do something else with my life.

"Kind of. It's not like I'm going there expecting him to just suddenly pop up after two years," I responded as something caught my eye moving toward us.

Narrowing both eyes into slits, I sighed as Myra stopped speaking to someone on her cell when her rounded orbs landed on me. She was as dressed down as I had ever seen her, with her hair slicked back into a bun at the nape of her neck and her baby hairs laid to perfection. She carried a garment bag over her shoulder as she approached. Tension instantly filled my body as my spine stiffened. When she paused beside our table, Shayne looked her up and down crazily and turned her nose up.

"Can we help you?" She immediately went into big sister mode since Myra was grilling the shit out of me.

Bentley approached from behind, but I put a hand up to stop him. I didn't want to make a scene, although it was clear from the blaze of fury behind her eyes that she was here for it.

"What can I do for you, Myra?"

"You think you got away with something, don't you?" Her raspy tone addressed me.

"I don't know what you're talking about." I shook my head.

"My son was delivered to me in a box! His throat was slit!" Myra screeched.

"Hmm, that's unfortunate," I muttered, bringing myself to my feet so I could go toe to toe with her. "What does that have to do with me?"

"He told me what he was doing the night he disappeared. I know he came to that club. He was with your hoe ass cousin. Her, that owner, and his girlfriend all died in that car accident, and my son ended up on my doorstep! None of that is a coincidence!" she hissed.

"You know what it's not? My problem, Myra. Your son was a sick, sadistic, son-of-a-bitch, and I have never slept better since knowing he isn't lurking around, ready to ruin my life." I sneered, causing her to lunge for me.

Both Bentley and Shayne appeared at my side, ready to defend me against her deranged ass.

"It's you standing here like he didn't deserve that shit for me. You know that nigga wasn't right in the head." I cackled, which only made her madder as she raised a hand.

Shayne caught her arm in the air and sent a punch across Myra's face.

"Don't touch my fucking sister!" she threatened. "Bentley, escort this bitch to the nearest exit."

He led Myra away, and she was holding her cheek while screaming obscenities in our direction the whole way. My eyes bucked as Shayne opened her hand to stretch her fingers while her face twisted in agony.

"Okay, see now, when my niece or nephew comes out swinging, you gon' know why." We burst out laughing together.

"Let's go."

We gathered our shopping bags and started toward the doors where we had parked.

That little encounter was entertaining. I wasn't worried about Myra by a long shot. If she wanted those kinds of problems, I was sure Wood wouldn't mind putting her in the dirt, just like her son.

Shayne and I walked to the fully loaded black Cadillac Escalade that Wylde had surprised her with. At first, she talked shit about how big it was, telling him it was a man's car, but she quickly shut the hell up when she got behind the wheel and started pushing it. She said it was her big boy toy, and she loved whipping that mothafucka through traffic because folks got out the way. Once we loaded our bags in the back, we both rounded the side of the car and hopped into our seats.

When we arrived at the house, I saw that Wood's car was parked, and Wylde's was right behind it. Before Shayne and I could even unload, both men came out of the house. Wylde was so chill and at home, rocking nothing but his jeans and wife beater as he approached Shayne and scooped her into a hug before they nastily tongued each other down. Wood walked up on me with a bowl of cereal and looking me up and down as I popped the back latch to access our bags.

"The fuck you doing provoking people, Lis?" I knew Bentley's ass was gon' snitch. Nigga was quiet as a church mouse, but reported my moves like the CIA.

"I didn't do shit. She was the one talking to me crazy. I just gave it right back. Anyway, fuck her."

"I'm trying to keep my body count down for the year, shorty. Too much shit already going on." He shook his head and took a mouthful of peanut butter Crunch.

I reached inside for some of the bags that I knew were mine.

"She started it, but I doubt I see her again anyway. I ain't worried about it."

"You damn sure ain't got shit to worry about," Wood assured me as he noticed me pulling more bags out and leaving them on the ground. "Did you leave anything in the damn mall? I hope you bought a nigga something."

"Oh, I did. It's something we both can enjoy." I nodded sexily, which gained a sexy grin from him as he bobbed his head.

"That's what I'm talking about. Yo, but go put that shit up and then take a ride with me. Misael is sleep, but Ledger said he would keep an eye on the other two," Wood instructed.

"Where are we going?"

"Too many questions, baby." That meant he was done talking to me.

He hated when I was curious, which usually meant he was about to surprise me, and Wood was a master at that. That nigga was really spoiling me to the point that another nigga would never be able to attempt a spot in my heart. It was reserved for him and only him from now until the casket dropped. Life with Wood was everything and then some.

Shayne helped me with the rest of the bags, along with Wylde until we were done. We hugged and said our goodbyes before they pulled away in their individual vehicles. Standing behind me, hands on my hips as he nudged me along to his waiting car, Wood pressed his semi hard dick into my ass and kissed my neck.

"So, other than shopping and the shit at the mall, how was your day?" he questioned, stopping to open the passenger door to his Audi for me.

"It was okay." I settled in the leather as he went to get in the driver's seat. "How are things going at the club?"

"Nothing I can't handle. Got the police department

breathing down my back about the shit with Merlin, D, and them bitches, but I ain't worried about it. Shit is all circumstancial. Ain't like shit can be proven. Merlin had a lot of enemies, and Yeva was drinking and driving in a very dangerous location." Wood started the car and casually lifted his shoulders.

"So, you don't think they have anything?"

"I know they don't or they wouldn't still be sniffing around. Don't worry about that shit," he insisted.

For a few minutes we cruised along the streets while J. Cole played softly. Occasionally, Wood would peer over at me. I was looking out of my window, trying to guess where he was taking me.

"We building a legacy, Lis. That's what we on, and if mothafuckas don't understand the vision, ain't nothing we can do for them." He continued to steer us along until we arrived on Renner Road.

There were a few office buildings on that block, along with a gas station and café. The area was being revamped after being shut down so long, and there were rows of old buildings that had been boarded up since I was a kid. The for-sale sign in front of one of them now had a bold sticker that read SOLD over the info now. Wood parked in front and shut the car off. He turned to me as my head swung toward the building and then back to him.

"What is this?"

"This is whatever you choose to make it." He leaned toward the middle console and propped his elbow on it as we studied the structure together. "I checked around and got this for damn near nothing. Working on the other buildings on this block. I even talked to some people on the city council about having an event to raise money and fix up the old library. We lining up sponsors to help get computers donated and other stuff to make the place more technologically friendly. You know all these kids with all that savvy shit. This is just the start of your vision." He dropped a set of keys in my hand and grinned.

Holding them tight in my palm, tears blinded me as I choked on the urge to burst into tears.

"I know it's not a lot, not right now, and its going to take some work, but you have a construction crew that will be working around the clock, along with an interior designer who won't make a move without you knowing. I gave them all your contact information. So, don't be surprised when they reach out, wanting to set up meetings and shit."

"Wood, I—" Gasping, I covered my mouth with both hands and cried.

"Aw shit, don't start that." His hand fell on the back of my neck, forcing me to look his way once again.

"I love you," I whispered, catching him off guard.

His eyes flickered before a sparkle lit them up.

I wasn't sure how I let those words slip. I just knew I meant them from the deepest part of my soul. His fingers caressed my scalp between my locs, and he sloped forward as his soft mouth crushed against mine in a passionate kiss. Our tongues danced like two old friends.

"I love you too." His dark eyes bounced around mine before he examined my mouth again and applied another sweet kiss.

Sometimes, it seemed like the nigga was too good to be true, but I was getting used to Wood just being who he was, a real ass nigga. He didn't mince words or pretend. If something was bothering him, he spoke on it. I was never left guessing with him, and I loved that more than anything. When we first got together, I thought he was brash and immature, but it was really just his personality. At his core, he was a big ass kid, but his heart was so big, even when he was trying to act like he didn't have one. I knew better.

"Come here." He urged me across the seat into his lap.

With my legs stretched across the middle into the other seat, I rested my head against his chest as his hand remained on my thigh. I admired the big ass rings that donned his fingers. He could pay a couple of salaries up for the year with the amount of ice they were covered in. Shit was ridiculous, but he loved wearing those big ass, flashy things. He cupped my chin between his thumb and first finger, forcing me to face him.

"You been a real one from the door, shorty, even when I was pretending this wasn't what it was. So, don't get it fucked up. A nigga ain't never met nobody like you before, Lis. To be real witchu, I didn't think a person like you existed. You bad, sexy as fuck, and you genuinely care about others before yourself. That fabric ain't even made no more. Shit obsolete out here, so don't ever let a mothafucka tell you otherwise."

I massaged the back of his neck while searching his eyes and smiling. He took my hand and intertwined our fingers before his mouth pressed against mine again and he fed me his tongue at the same time. His phone buzzing in his pocket pulled us apart. Wood dug it out and stared at the screen. His father was calling.

"I don't even want to deal with this nigga," he muttered.

"What's wrong?"

"Him and Wylde on some other shit, and I ain't trying to be in the middle of it. They need to work that out without me."

"Maybe you can give them middle ground." I suggested, tugging on his ear before kissing his cheek.

"I don't know about all that. They some hotheads separately," Wood acknowledged.

I could tell the subject really bothered him as his phone rang once more. It was his father again. Sighing heavily, he swiped to pick up and mashed the phone against his ear.

"What's up, Pop?" Wood asked after putting it on speaker.

"I need to talk to you and Wylde. We have some family

business that needs to be addressed immediately. Tomorrow night, six pm, Vaughn's Grill," he listed off.

"Yeah, okay. I'll inform Wylde and Richie as well." His father declared before hanging up.

"What was that about?" I questioned.

"Who the fuck knows?" Shaking his head, he dropped his phone in the console and swiped his hand down his face. "Whatever it is, I'm sure it's not good."

The next day, Shayne and I met up after making sure the kids were good with Nael and loaded up with Bentley to go visit Miles. Misael was getting more easily fatigued these days, and getting around less, which was normal. When he was first diagnosed, they only gave him a couple of years to live anyway. It ended up being five since then, and he was still alive and kicking. I was grateful for it, but time was ticking, and I could see it in his eyes with every passing day. The doctors said he wasn't getting any better, and the cancer was spreading even faster. We were discussing hospice options for him to keep him comfortable since he could no longer even get around in his wheelchair. Surprisingly, it was Ledger who had stepped up to be there for him the most.

"What you thinking about?" Shayne's voice pried me from my dark thoughts, and I swung my head toward her.

Forcing a smile on my lips, I fought tears. "Misael. He's getting so weak. I'm such a mess with hormones that I can't even be around him for long without wanting to fall apart. I'm acting like he hasn't lived a long life."

"He's dying, Lis. It's going to hurt either way." Shayne sympathized as she reached for my hand. "You know I'm here for you."

"I know." I bowed my head. "We have known for a while now that it was coming. I just didn't think it would hurt like this. He's all I have left of family like that. Despite everything Leslie was, at the end of the day, she was still his daughter. He's my grandpa, and we haven't always seen eye to eye, but I respect him. I just hope he knows that."

"I'm sure he does. He has to respect you too, though. I mean, look at everything you've done for your family, Lishan. You could have walked out a long time ago and left him with the kids, but you didn't."

"I have to be there for them now, too. He's a mean old man, but they love him. I do too."

About an hour later, we pulled in front of the care facility in Manhattan, and Bentley opened the door for us to get out. Shayne pulled the Champion windbreaker around her and adjusted her tote on her shoulder. We were both dressed down as we took the sidewalk to the revolving doors not far away. The weather was starting to warm up, so the air wasn't all icy like the past few months. Bentley said he was going to park and would join us inside, so we ducked in from the brisk day and signed in. The place seemed a little busy with people passing by or going outside with their elders, walking them around and talking to them. The area where they could watch TV had drawn a lot of them today as well.

After we placed our nametags on to show who we were visiting, Shayne led me to a set of elevators a couple of steps away. We waited for one to land on our floor, and seconds later, we climbed on. I was so nervous that I was wringing my clammy hands together and bouncing from foot to foot. Snickering, with her eyes on the numbers at the top of the car, showing what floor we were on, Shayne glanced my way.

"You're acting like he's awake. Relax."

"I can't help it. You never know your father and then try to picture him and see how that goes. I know you showed me a couple of pictures, and you said he and Nael look alike, but... it's different actually meeting him and seeing him in person."

We landed on the fifth floor, and when we got off, Shayne paused. The elevator doors slid closed behind us, but she pressed a hand against the wall and rested it there as her other hand lay on her stomach.

"You okay?" I checked with her, she seemed unsettled.

"Yeah." She nodded, and we took a left while searching the names on the doors.

We arrived outside the door to room 511, and the name, Rogan, Miles was on a nameplate. She glanced my way before turning the handle and pushing the door open. There was a couch and dresser in front of us as soon as we entered, and on top were a bunch of framed pictures and fresh flowers in a vase. A leather recliner was in the farthest corner, and there was a TV mounted to the wall above the dresser. The bed hadn't come into view yet, and we both stepped inside the average sized, dimly lit room. There were a couple of windows, and the blinds and curtains hadn't been opened today. Unsure what to expect, when goosebumps prickled my arms, I froze. Shayne approached the side of the bed where a figure lay.

"Hey, old man." Her soft voice echoed off the walls as she stopped, and her posture suddenly went rigid.

Lingering near the foot of the small bed, something seemed off as I scoped the rest of the room. A shadow moved swiftly, and the door suddenly closed so hard it jolted my entire body. Shayne also jumped, and we spun simultaneously as the devil himself appeared.

"What's up, baby mama?" Elim's wicked grin sent Shayne's eyes bucking as the urge to piss on myself sent a paralyzing fear throughout my bones.

Wylde

Later that day...

"Yo, what you think this about?" Wood dug into his salad while I brought the glass of whiskey I had been nursing to my lips.

We were seated in a small Italian restaurant surrounded by a bunch of uppity mothafuckas I didn't know or care for. My phone buzzed in my pocket, and it was a message coming through from Shayne. Her name had been upgraded in my phone to *Wife,* and I smiled while skimming her text. She and Lishan were on their way to see her pops, so she was letting me know they were heading that way. I was glad that situation had worked out the way it did. At first, I wasn't sure how shorty was going to take the news, and it did seem to rock her, but she loved Lishan already, so it made the transition a hell of a lot easier.

"Knowing Waker, ain't no telling," I responded, shaking my head.

I responded to Shayne's text telling her to be safe and I would see her later at home. It was wild when I thought about how far we had come. It was hard to fathom that we hadn't known each other prior to a couple of months ago. I couldn't imagine life without her or the kids.

Looking up, I spotted our father heading our way. His expression and posture were stern in the blue suit and white button up shirt he wore. He pulled out the chair across from me and my brother and settled in. When a waitress approached, I ordered another drink, and so did Pop.

"I'm surprised you're both on time." Waker unbuttoned his suit jacket and eased back in his seat.

"The fuck is this about?" Any patience I had was thin as thread as I reclined and twirled my glass on the table.

"Let's wait until all parties are here." Just as those words left his lips, Rich pulled up behind him. It was obvious from the sharp stares they cut toward each other that they weren't seeing eye to eye. Rich dropped down in the chair beside me and across from Wood.

"Nice of you to join us, Richie. I didn't think you would show up," Waker taunted as he guzzled his bourbon.

"What's the deal? Why are we here, Pop?" Wood wiped his mouth with his napkin and reached for his glass of lemon water.

"I met with the board. Seems you all are pretty preoccupied. They had some concerns." My father's posture was upright, haughty as his dark eyes took us all in, one by one.

"You met with the board but didn't bother to notify the remaining members?" I asked, still twirling my glass as resentment built in my chest.

"It seems a lot of them have concerns about the future of the company. Your associations with organized crime, and everything in between. We had a nice, long, chat. I have gained the majority vote, regardless of how any of you sway. So, Wylde, you will be my right hand. Wood, what is it you do these days?" Waker fixed his gaze on his youngest son.

"That's fucked up, Waker." Wood shook his head as Rich and I remained fixated on him with hatred resonating in our eyes.

I wasn't sure which of us was more pissed, but the way his hands locked together let me know he was keeping himself from putting hands on this nigga just like I was. Leaning forward, I swallowed the rest of my whiskey and slammed the glass on the table.

"You think this shit is a game or something? The fuck makes you think you can come in and make those kinds of calls?" I demanded, brows knitting together like a bridge across my forehead.

"I fall in line before you. It's called seniority—"

"It's called being a snake ass mothafucka," I corrected through gritted teeth.

"Waker, the fuck—" Rich's tone was even as he stroked his beard and sighed.

"You told me to figure it out, remember? You didn't want to let me in, Rich. You failed to realize I have just as much right to all of this as you and both of them." Waker waved a finger over the three of us. "More, actually, big brother. The shareholders agreed that someone should take over. Someone who won't be distracted. There are concerns about personal relationships within the atmosphere and how it's giving us a reputation for not having our shit in order." He pointedly responded, aiming his orbs at me first and then Wood.

I was so livid I was ready to reach across the table and snatch him out of that fucking chair. It was one thing when he ran things into the ground in LA, and I had to step in. I gave him the benefit of the doubt back then because I knew he was also grieving. Now, he was liable to get sent to the crossroads fucking with me.

"So, you staged a coup? Now what? We can still meet with the shareholders ourselves," Rich chimed in.

"You could, true. Won't change the outcome, though. They have all pretty much made up their minds. The organizational announcement is being drawn up as we speak. Everyone will know that I am in charge and will answer to me. First order of business is weeding some of these agents out that aren't bringing anything to the table. We need to have more in the field time. I also plan to enforce a strict policy on dating in the office atmosphere. He explained. "As for you two, it's time to think about the future and what you are putting out there as Katri men. We get married, we have families, we—"

"Lie and cheat?" I suggested, catching him off guard with my harsh tone as he paused mid-sentence and shot daggers across the table at me. "Or how about abandoning our families when shit gets hard? Is that what we want to instill?"

"Hate me all you want, Wylde, but I'm the reason you are the man you are today, nigga. Don't you ever forget that!" he hissed.

I lunged out of my seat, snatching him up roughly by the collar of his blazer and dragging him across the table so I could bring my face as close to his as possible. Looking into his shadowy orbs triggered something inside that snapped in two as I realized my own reflection gaped back at me through that cold stare. He was right. With my jaw locked tight, I grunted and shoved him out of my grasp. He fumbled a little in his chair but managed to stay sitting up as he pulled his jacket and smoothed it out against his muscular frame. Yeah, he might have been an older man, but much like Rich, Waker kept himself in shape and visited the gym regularly. He wasn't chiseled down, but he was in shape and managed to still get around like someone half his age.

"Calm down, bro." Wood had stood when I snatched Waker up, but he placed a hand against my chest in an effort to calm me as I bit into my bottom lip with fury.

The hatred boiling in me was sure to bubble over. Clearing his throat, Waker stood and swallowed the remaining alcohol in his glass before he set it back on the table.

"I guess I will see y'all Monday morning. Make sure you're on time. Oh, and make sure the women in your life are also in attendance. I don't want to repeat myself."

He turned to go, and I was ready to charge and take him to the ground, but Rich nodded to my chair, advising me to take a seat as Wood lowered himself back into his. Pinching the bridge of my nose, I took in a few deep breaths and released them as our waiter came over to clear Wood's plate. She asked if she could get us anything else. and I ordered another damn drink, and so did my uncle.

"He can't just do that shit, can he?" Wood questioned once we were alone and absorbing what the fuck had happened.

"I always knew he was a fuck nigga, especially after Ma died, but this shit." I shook my head, and Rich tightened up at my side while gazing straight ahead.

"Waker plays dirty. He always has. Don't worry about him. Let him get comfortable. Allow him to think he's running shit for now. I'll find out what he has on the other shareholders. It has to be something that got them all to turn. I don't think it was just his manipulation. The fact that you two have been the source of so much attention lately probably ain't helping matters," Rich conveyed. "Don't play into it, Wylde. He wants a reaction from you. It will just be another way for him to make you look bad. Waker been doing this shit his whole fucking life and getting away with it."

"So, we supposed to sit around and let him fuck shit up because his ego and pride are bruised?"

"He always hangs himself. You just gotta give him enough rope," Rich pointed out.

"What's the history there?" I pried, noticing Rich immediately fill with tension as he eased back against the iron of the chair he sat in.

"Long. Sordid. I vowed to never bring you or Wood into our shit. It was easier when y'all were in LA," he mumbled as our drinks were brought over.

"Easier to lie?" I questioned with a lifted brow.

"I never wanted to be the reason your relationship with your father changed. You had to be the one to figure out who he was, who you were, and what you wanted for yourself. I always told you that, right?" Rich presented.

"Yeah, and Pop always resented you for it," Wood replied.

"He had his reasons. None of the shit had to do with either of you. Things between me and Waker been off for a long time. Don't let him get under your skin. You just got here, and I know you both got a lot on your plate—"

"Nah, not enough to not handle this." I moved my head back and forth while taking my glass between my fingers again.

I was so angry that I wasn't even feeling this shit as the warm liquid coursed through me.

"I'm in town for a few more days. Let me talk to some people, see what kind of promises he made, and get back with you. This ain't over."

Guzzling the last of my drink, I took a peek at the Patek on my wrist and saw that it was almost seven-thirty.

I was going to head home and spend some one on one time with the kids until Shayne got back. After paying the tab, me, Wood and Rich all started toward the main entrance together. That nagging pull I'd had all day started to go off. My senses tingled as we neared the doors to the restaurant. Stepping out front, I adjusted my blazer as Wood stepped out on one side and Rich took my right.

"Excuse me." A woman's voice pulled all our attention just past Wood.

This little thick shorty with jet black hair past her shoulders, a middle part, and keen cocoa brown orbs zoomed in on my brother. She was in jeans, a tank top, and a cardigan over the look that matched the olive green boots on her feet. Attitude was stretched across her face as she draped an arm over the little nigga she had rolled up on us with. The whole situation had me frowning right along with my brother as he carefully raked his eyes over her.

"I know you?" Wood checked with her.

She smacked her lips before giving an eye roll. "You probably don't remember me. My name is Sunniva. I'm Noemi's sister," she introduced herself in a raspy voice.

Her plush lips were glossy as hell, making it hard to focus on her other attributes.

Wood nodded at the mention before eyeing the little man who was staring him down.

"Okay, so what can I do for you?" he asked, hands jammed into his pockets as he carefully sized her up.

I didn't know what kind of time she was on, but she didn't seem like much of a threat to me. The wind blew, shifting the air, and my heart raced as large goosebumps prickled the back of my neck, causing my hairs to rise as well. When my phone buzzed in my pocket, I reached in and studied the screen as *Wife* popped up again. Swiping the bar, I put it to my ear.

"What's up, mama?" I asked, squinting as something moving above caught my eye.

"Wylde." Shayne sniffled into the phone, and I knew instantly that something was wrong.

My blood turned cold, making the air around me toxic. Everything was moving simultaneously. I spun as Sunniva placed a hand on each shoulder of the little man and positioned him in front of her. Little nigga was about as tall as her, and there was something familiar in his eyes as they examined Wood.

"This is Wise. He's your son," Sunniva calmly stated.

"The fuck you say?" Squinting, he took a step closer, and she cowered back some as her revelation hit us all.

"Wylde..." Shayne's voice pulled me from the scene in front of me as something glinted off a streetlight.

I realized what the movement was across the street from the rooftop.

"Shit!" I hissed as the spark went off, and the bullet whizzed through the air toward me.

I reeled with shock as Rich dove in front of me, shielding me from the shell. It struck him instead and sent him falling into me. We both hit the ground and this scorching burn seared my side. I knocked my head against the concrete, and pain traveled through me. Trying to take in a breath, Rich's lips moved, but it was obvious from the agony in his eyes that he couldn't get the words out.

"Fuck, Rich!" Peering down, I saw all the blood as his eyes bore into mine, glistening in torture as his tongue finally allowed him to speak.

"You... are... my son," were his last words before his breath was stolen from him, and he collapsed against my chest.

The fuck?

To Be Continued...

Also by S.L. Partee

Plan B Drama & Baby Mama's

Made in United States
North Haven, CT
24 January 2024